A Stitch in Time

PENELOPE LIVELY

E. P. Dutton & Co., Inc.   New York

To Joy, Max, Tim and Nick

First published in the U.S.A. 1976 by E. P. Dutton
Copyright © 1976 by Penelope Lively

Library of Congress Cataloging in Publication Data

Lively, Penelope   A stitch in time

SUMMARY: A quiet lonely child spending her holidays by
the sea is changed by an inexplicable link with people
and events of one hundred years ago and also by the
very real and lively family next door.
[1. Space and time—Fiction]   I. Title.

PZ7.L7397St3   [Fic]   76-23118   ISBN 0-525-40040-0

Printed in the U.S.A.   First Edition
10 9 8 7 6 5 4 3 2 1

Contents

A House, a Cat and Some Fossils

'All right, back there?' said Maria's father.

'Not much longer now,' said Maria's mother.

Neither of them turned round. The backs of their heads rode smoothly forward between the landscapes that unrolled at either side of the car; hedges, trees, fields, houses that came and went before there was time to examine them. Fields with corn. Fields with animals. From time to time, on the left, snatches of a milky green sea bordered with a ribbon of golden sand or shingle. That is the English Channel, said Maria, inside her head, to the ashtray on the back of the car seat, the sea. We have come to spend our summer holiday beside it, because that is what people do. You go down to the beach every day and run about and shout and build sandcastles and all that. You have blown-up rubber animals and iced lollies and there is sand in your bed at night. You do that in August. As far as I know everybody in the world does.

The car slowed down and turned into the forecourt of a garage. 'QUAD GREEN SHIELD STAMPS!' screamed the garage, 'WINEGLASS OFFER! JIGSAWS! GREAT PAINTINGS OF THE WORLD!'

'Just short of three hours,' said Mr Foster. 'Not bad.'

'Quite good traffic,' said Mrs Foster.

They both turned round now to look at Maria, with kindly smiles.

'You're very quiet.'

'Not feeling sick or anything?'

Maria said she was quite all right and she wasn't feeling sick. She watched her father get out of the car and start to fill it with petrol from the pump. He was wearing a special, new, holiday shirt. She could tell it was a holiday shirt because it had red and blue stripes. His shirts for ordinary life were never striped. On the far side of the petrol pump another car drew up. It was full of children, most of them small and several of them wailing. A boy of about Maria's age looked at her for a moment through the window, his expression irritable and bored. A woman got out of the car, saying loudly, 'Now just shut up for a moment, the lot of you.'

Maria stared at the face of the petrol pump. It had a benevolent face, if you discounted a bright orange sticker across its forehead, which referred to the Wineglass Offer.

'Noisy lot,' said the petrol pump. 'You get all kinds, this time of year.'

'I expect you do,' said Maria. 'It'll be your busy season, I should imagine.'

'Too right,' said the petrol pump. 'It's all go. Rushed off my feet, I am, if you see what I mean.' In the other car, the two youngest children had struck up a piercing argument about who had kicked whom, and the petrol pump spluttered as it clocked up the next gallon, 'Excuse me . . . It goes right through my head, that racket. Personally I prefer a nice quiet child. You're just the one, are you?'

'That's right,' said Maria, 'I'm an only.'

'Very nice too,' said the petrol pump, 'I daresay. Had a good journey down?'

'Not bad,' said Maria. 'We had quite good traffic.'

'I'll tell you where you get good traffic,' said the petrol pump with animation. 'The coast road on a Saturday night. Nose to tail all the way. Spectacular. Now that's what I call traffic.'

'We get good rush-hours,' said Maria, 'where we live. On the edge of London.'

'Is that so? Jammed solid—that kind of thing?'

There was no time for more. Maria's father got into the car again and started the engine.

'Cheerio,' said the petrol pump. 'Nice meeting you. All the best. Take care. Don't do anything I wouldn't.'

'Right you are,' said Maria. 'Thanks for the petrol.'

'You're welcome.'

Back behind her parents' travelling heads, with Dorset unrolling tidily at each side of her, Maria hoped there would be something to talk to at this holiday house her parents had rented for the month. You can always talk to people, of course. It's usual, indeed. The trouble with people is that they expect you to say particular things, and so you end up saying what they expect, or want. And they usually end up saying what you expected them to. Grown-ups, Maria had noticed, spent much time telling each other what the weather was like, or wondering aloud if one thing would happen, or another. She herself quite liked to talk to her mother, but somehow her mother was always about to go out, or into another room, and by the time Maria had got to the point of the conversation, she had gone. Her father when she talked to him would listen with distant kindliness, but not as though what she said were of any great importance. Which, of course, it might not be. Except, she thought, to me. And so for real conversations, Maria considered, things were infinitely preferable. Animals, frequently. Trees and plants, from time to time. Sometimes what they said was consoling, and sometimes it was uncomfortable, but at least you were having a conversation. For a real heart-to-heart you couldn't do much better than a clock. For a casual chat almost anything would do.

'A holiday house,' she said to the ashtray, 'is presumably bright pink or something. Not normal at all. With balloons tied to the windows and a funny hat on the chimney. And jolly music coming out of the walls.'

'Here we are,' said Mrs Foster, and as she spoke Maria saw this place announce itself with a road-sign. Lyme Regis. She had been

3

studying road-signs throughout the journey. The places to which one was not going were always the most enticing, lying secretly to right and left out of sight beyond fields and hills, promised by sign-posts that lured you with their names—Sixpenny Handley, Winterborne Stickland, Piddletrenthide and Affpuddle. They seemed not quite real. Could they be like other places, with bungalows, primary schools and a Post Office? Like the green tracks that plunged off between hedges and fields, they invited you to find out. And I'll never know now, she thought sadly. That's one of the lots of things I'll never know.

She turned her attention to Lyme Regis, which she would have to know, like it or not. It did not seem too bad. It did not, for instance, have houses in rows. Maria had quite strong opinions about a fair number of things, though she seldom mentioned them to anyone, and she did not care for places in which houses were lined up in rows, staring blankly at you as you passed, though in fact she lived in this kind of house herself, and so did everyone she knew. The houses in this town, on the whole, were differently arranged. Their problem, if you could call it that, was that the town was built upon a hillside, or several hillsides, and seemed in grave danger of slithering down into the sea, so that each house had to dig its toes in, as it were, bracing itself against the slope with walls and ledges and gardens. The houses rose one above another, lifting roofs and chimneys and windows out of the green embrace of trees. She had never seen a place with so many trees, big ones and little ones, light and dark, all different. And between them you could see slices of a sparkling sea, tipped here and there with the white fleck of waves.

'Delightful,' said Mrs Foster.

'Nice Victorian atmosphere,' said Mr Foster. And then, 'This must be it, I think.'

They turned into a gravelled drive, tightly lined with bright green hedge. The drive made a little flourish between hedge and a somewhat unkempt shrubbery, and then ended up in front of a house.

4

Maria and her parents got out of the car and stood in front of the house, considering it. At least Maria considered it. Her mother said, 'How pretty. I like the white stucco,' and her father began to take the suitcases from the car. Maria went on considering.

It was a tidy house. It did not sprawl, as some of its neighbours sprawled, into such follies as little towers and turrets, glassed-in verandas, porches and protrusions of one kind and another. It stood neat and square—or rather, rectangular, for it was longer than it was high—with a symmetrical number of green-shuttered windows upstairs and down, at either side of a black front door with a fan-light above it. Its only frivolity was a pale green iron canopy with a frilled edge that ran the length of the house just beneath the upstairs windows.

'Well, Maria,' said Mr Foster. 'Is it anything like you imagined?'

'No,' said Maria.

'About 1820, I should think,' said Mr Foster, in his instructing voice. 'That kind of architecture is called Regency.'

And Maria thought, never mind about that, because somewhere there's a swing. It's blowing in the wind—I can hear the squeaking noise it makes. Good, I shall like having my own swing. And someone's got a little dog, that keeps yapping. She walked round the corner of the house into the garden, to see where this swing might be, but there was nothing to be seen except a large square lawn, edged with more dense and shaggy shrubbery and a good many trees. At the end of the garden was a hedge, and beyond that the hillside dropped away steeply down towards the sea. The sun had gone in now, and the glitter was gone from the sea. Instead it reached away upwards to the sky, grey-green splashed here and there with white, to melt into a grey-blue sky so gently that it was hard to tell where one began and the other ended. To right and left the coast stretched away in a haze of greens and golds and misty blues, and immediately in front of the town a stone wall curled out into the sea to put a protective arm round a little harbour filled with resting boats, their masts like rows of toothpicks. Gulls floated to and fro across the harbour, and on the beach behind it people sat in clumps and dogs skittered in and out of the water. It was a view you could spend much time examining.

The swing, she decided, must be in the adjoining garden, which was almost completely hidden by trees. The house next door, which was large, and of the towered and turreted kind, could just be seen between them. She went back to the front of the house again, where her father was just unlocking the door. They went inside.

'Good grief!' said Mrs Foster 'It's the real thing! Stopped dead in 1880.'

Whereas outside all had been softly coloured—green and blue and gold—within the house all was solidly brown. The walls, in the hall at least, were panelled. A brown clock ticked upon a table over which was spread a brown velvet tablecloth ('Tassels and all,' said Mrs Foster, picking up one edge and letting it drop again. 'My!'). A brownly patterned carpet was spread across part of the brown tiled floor. Thick brown curtains hung at either side of the french windows opening on to the garden, visible through the door of what was clearly the main room. (This, said Maria to herself, is what is called a drawing-room, like they have in books and I have never seen before.) They all three walked into this room, and stood for a moment in silence.

'The drawing-room, I should imagine,' said Maria's mother.

Bulbous chairs and small, uncomfortable-looking sofas stood about, confronting one another. A vast piano was shrouded in a brown cover made to fit it. On the mantelpiece, stuffed birds sat dejectedly on twigs beneath a glass dome: they seemed, at first glance, to be sparrows but would be worth further investigation, Maria thought. I could look them up, she decided hopefully. She liked looking things up. Perhaps they would turn out to be rare warblers, or something extinct.

They toured the room. On one wall was a huge brown oil painting

6

of a man in Highland costume standing in front of a mountain, surrounded by a great many dead birds and animals. A glass-fronted cabinet stood against another wall, crammed with china ornaments. A bookcase was filled from top to bottom with books that tidily matched one another, all their spines lettered in gold. You could never, Maria thought, never never take a book like that to bed with you. Or read it in the lavatory. You would have to sit on one of those hard-looking chairs, wearing your best clothes, with clean hands.

'Well,' said Mrs Foster, 'what do you think of it?'

'I hadn't thought,' said Maria, 'that a holiday house would be like this.'

'To be frank,' said her father, 'neither had I.'

They inspected the rest of the house. Downstairs there was a dining-room, in which eight leather-seated chairs were gathered round a very long table. Above the sideboard hung another brown oil painting in which dead hares, rabbits and pheasants were spread artistically across a chair. There was a further room, which Maria instantly identified (to herself) as a study, lined with bookcases from floor to ceiling and furnished with more brown chairs and sofas. The kitchen was relatively normal. Upstairs there were several bedrooms and a bathroom. The bath, Maria noted with delight, had feet shaped like an animal's claws. She considered it for some time before following her parents down the stairs again.

As they reached the hall once more there was a sudden disturbance. The fringed cloth upon the table twitched, and from under it emerged a large tabby cat, which strode into the middle of the carpet and sat staring at them for a moment. Then it set about washing its face.

'Fully furnished seems to include resident cat,' said Mr Foster. 'Nobody said anything about that.'

The cat yawned and wandered out of the open front door. It cast a speculative look at the car and stalked off into a shrubbery.

Mr and Mrs Foster became active and business-like, unloading the

7

car, carrying things into the house and investigating the cooker and the electrical appliances, which seemed to be firmly of the twentieth century. Maria followed them around, helping when asked.

'Which room would you like, darling? This one, with the view of the sea?'

Maria went to the window. It was the same view of sea and harbour, horizon and cloud, that she had studied from the garden, with, this time, the garden itself in front. The window rattled in a gust of wind and again she thought she heard a swing squeak.

'Yes, please,' she said.

The room itself was small, and much filled with furniture—little round tables with frilled edges, a rather high large bed with brass rails at head and foot, many sombre pictures, and, on one of the tables, a miniature chest about eighteen inches high with many small drawers. Maria opened one, and was confronted with three rows of bluish-grey fossils, like little ridged wheels, neatly arranged on faded brown stuff like felt and labelled in small meticulous handwriting. *Promicroceras planicosta,* she read. *Asteroceras obtusum.*

'Well,' said her mother. 'We'd better get the cases up. Are you coming?'

'In a minute,' said Maria.

She closed the drawer of the chest, deciding to save the fossils until later. She got up on the bed and bounced. It was lumpy but somehow embracing. The big chest of drawers was empty and smelled of moth-balls. She turned to the window and looked out into the garden. There was a huge dark tree at one side of it that she had not noticed before, a very solid and ancient-looking tree, quite different from the more ordinary and recognizable ones that swayed and shook in the sea wind. The garden seemed to perch on the hillside, suspended above the sea, a bare, rather neglected garden, with hardly any flowers. The trees and shrubberies, though, were inviting. They would have to be explored.

The cat brushed its way into the room, making her jump and

8

stumble against one of the small tables. An ornament fell to the floor. She picked it up and saw guiltily that it was chipped. She put it back on the table.

'Fool,' said the cat.

'What?'

'Fool, I said. I suppose you think you'll get away with that.'

'I might,' said Maria.

The cat yawned. 'Possibly,' it said. 'And again possibly not.' It licked one paw delicately, sitting in a patch of sunlight.

'I must say you've got some very attractive Victorian atmosphere here,' said Maria.

'We aim to please,' said the cat.

'Where's the swing?' Maria asked.

'There isn't one.'

'Yes, there is. I heard it squeaking.'

'Have it your own way,' said the cat. 'You'll soon find out.' It squinted at her through half-closed eyes and went on, 'And don't maul me about. I can't stand it. The last lot were forever patting and stroking. "Nice pussy, dear pussy." Ugh!'

'I don't like cats,' said Maria.

'And I'm not keen on children. How old are you? Nine?'

'Eleven,' said Maria coldly.

'Bit small, aren't you?'

'That's not my fault.'

'Rather on the plain side, too, I'd say. Mousy. Not like that Caroline next door to you at home. Her with the long fair hair. And the two sisters she's always rushing about with. Laughing and pushing each other.'

'You would know about Caroline,' said Maria.

The cat inspected its paw, and stretched. 'Is your mother a good cook?'

'Very,' said Maria.

'Lavish helpings? Plenty of scraps left—that kind of thing?'

'I should think you'll be all right.'

'Good,' said the cat. 'Last week was a bit thin. Big family. Everyone after the pickings. There's a lot to be said for a small litter.' It eyed Maria thoughtfully, 'Or don't you agree?'

'You can't be sure,' said Maria, 'when you are. You don't know what it would be like otherwise. They nearly didn't have me, you know. I heard my mother say so once to her friend. But they're glad they did now.'

'Is that so?' said the cat. 'Fancy.' It sounded unconvinced. 'Well, I'll be seeing you, no doubt.' It sauntered out of the room and down the stairs, its tail waving elegantly from side to side.

With their possessions spread around the house—paperback books on the tables in the drawing-room, groceries in the kitchen, coats in the hall—its strong personality began to seem a little diluted. It became slightly more docile, as though it belonged to them instead of being entirely independent. They ate their lunch in the kitchen: somehow the dining-room seemed too forbidding, at least for cold pork pies and salad. The cat came in and fawned for a while against Mrs Foster's legs, until fed some scraps. Toady, said Maria to it silently, sucker-up . . . It gave her a baleful stare and settled down to sleep beside the cooker.

The last tenants of the house had left evidence of themselves in the form of half-emptied packets of cereals on the kitchen shelf (Rice Krispie people they had been, Maria noted, with one family rebel who favoured Frosties), a plastic duck under the bath, a shredded burst balloon and some comics in the waste-paper basket in her room, some bits of Lego down the side of the drawing-room sofa and a battered fork-lift truck behind the cooker. Mrs Foster swept all these objects up and threw them into the dustbin. Maria regretted this: she had been trying to imagine from them what this invisible family might have been like. They seemed to have been of mixed ages and sexes. The house, she thought, must have been noisy last week. It was very quiet now, after lunch, as her mother washed up, her father read the newspaper, and she stood looking out into the garden.

'Shall we go and see what the beach is like?'

'Yes, please,' said Maria.

The beach that they went to was a couple of miles or so from the town. Maria, with several years' experience of beaches behind her, found herself instantly awarding it a high mark. It was unassuming, to begin with—a row of beach huts being about the only facilities it offered. And the clutches of people spread fairly thickly over the area near the car park and beach huts soon thinned out so that to either side the beach stretched away more and more uncluttered, with just a dog or child scampering at the water's edge, or family group encamped against the cliff.

It was the cliffs that instantly attracted her attention. Again, they made no large claims: not for them the craggy grandeurs of Cornwall or Wales. And they looked, in some indefinable way, soft rather than hard. It was the colour, chiefly, the slaty grey-blue that matched so nearly the now clouded sky, so that the sea, which had changed from milky green to a pale turquoise, lay as a belt of colour between the grey cliffs, the bright shingle of the beach, and the grey sky. And yet they were not, she saw, the same colour all the way up. They were capped at the top with a layer of golden-brown, which in turn was finished off with a green skin of vegetation. And here and there the three levels of colour became confused and inter-mixed, where grass and trees and bushes apparently tumbled in a green tongue down the face of the cliff. She stood staring, entranced, at this agreeable place where Dorset ends, and England, and both slide gracefully away into the sea.

'Here, I think,' said Mrs Foster. They spread their rug and sat.

They were sitting, as Maria soon found, upon more than just a slab of this grey-blue stone. In the first place it was not stone at all, but a hard, dry clay. A piece of it flaked off under her fingers, as she scratched idly at it. And then, looking closer, lying on her stomach with her face a few inches above the rock, it came to life suddenly under her very eyes. For it was inhabited. There, like delicate scribblings upon the clay, were the whirls and spirals of shell-like creatures—the same, she recognized, as those in the miniature chest of drawers in her room back at that house. But smaller, these were, barely an inch or so across, some of them, but perfect in each ridge and twist. And as she prised one out with the edge of a shell it crumbled between her fingers into blue dust, but there, below and beneath, was another, and another, and another. The whole rock streamed with a petrified ghost-life.

'Look,' said Maria.

'Fossils,' said her mother. 'Ammonites. This coast is famous for fossils. You could collect them.' She settled herself on her back, a hump of jerseys under her head, and turned the page of her book.

But I don't want to spoil these any more, Maria thought. They're so pretty. And they've been there for millions and millions of years so it's stupid to spend a Friday afternoon now picking them out and breaking them. If I was good at drawing I would draw a picture of them.

Instead, she examined the rock carefully, to remember it, and then wandered off among the neighbouring rocks to see if there were any more the same. Most were smooth and empty but one or two glinted with this remote life, though less lavishly. And then she found that by exploring carefully among the pebbles and chunks of rock with which this part of the beach was littered she could collect fossil fragments, like sections of small grey wheels, and occasionally a small, complete, flat one. Once she found a slab of the blue-grey stone, nine or ten inches across, in which two of the fossils hung one above another—ghostly creatures suspended in the small chunk of a solidified ancient sea that she held between her hands. She wrapped it in her anorak to take back with her.

Late in the afternoon they walked back to the car park along a beach from which the sea had retreated, leaving huge expanses of glistening sand on which children ran and shouted. At the edge of the distant water sea birds scurried to and fro before the waves. People were gathering themselves together, picking up buckets, spades, picnic baskets, folding chairs. What are beaches like at night, Maria wondered, all empty . . .

'I expect you'll soon make some friends down here,' said her mother.

'Yes, I expect so,' said Maria, without conviction.

Back at the house, in the privacy of her room, she laid the fossils out on the chest. It did not seem her room yet. Last week, after all, someone else had called it their room, and a week or two before that, someone else. It felt impersonal—not quite rejecting her, but not welcoming either. The fossils, she felt, might establish her in some way. I will get a book about fossils, she thought, and see what kind they are, and put labels on them like that other person did once, who found the ones in the miniature chest of drawers. Had that person, she wondered, collected them from that same stretch of beach? They were much superior to her broken fragments. Taking them out of the drawers to examine more carefully, one by one, she heard the squeak of that swing again, and went to the window to see if she could see it in the next-door garden. Trees, though, blocked the view.

Her father came along the passage and stopped at the open door of the room.

'Well, then . . . All settled in?'

'Yes,' said Maria. Her father was older than most people's fathers; he was beginning to go bald, his hair forming a neat horse-shoe around his scalp. He had changed from his holiday shirt into a special holiday sweater, she noticed. They looked at each other, as they often did, both wondering what to say next.

'Explored everything by now, I expect,' said Mr Foster.

'I haven't seen all of the garden yet.'

Mr Foster looked out into the garden with faint alarm, as though it might make demands of him. In London they had no garden.

'Yes,' he said. 'Well, I daresay it could come in useful.'

There was silence. 'Well,' said Mr Foster, 'I suppose it's about time for supper.' He went downstairs.

They spent a quiet evening, going early to bed. Maria, feeling drugged by wind and sea, slept soundly, woken only once by some small dog that barked shrilly from somewhere outside.

2

An Ilex Tree and a Boy

The garden, she discovered the next day, had possibilities. Without flower-beds, and furnished entirely with trees and shrubs that were clearly more or less indestructible, it was not at all the kind of garden in which you are being forever told not to step on the flowers or climb the trees. The huge, dank shrubbery that separated it from the next-door garden was a rabbit-warren of leafy tunnels and tents, inviting games of one kind or another. The trouble was that there was no one to play them with. Maria crawled aimlessly through and around. Then she turned to tree-climbing. One tree in particular attracted attention. It was the big dark tree she had noticed from the window, thickly leaved with shiny dark green leaves, and with massive trunk and branches grey-ribbed like the limbs of an elephant. It was a most majestic tree, and moreover designed just right for climbing, with branches that led on enticingly one from another, and met the trunk in ample curves that made natural sitting places. One, she found, was a perfect armchair vantage-point, not too alarmingly far above the ground, but commanding a view through the leaves into the next-door garden.

She sat there, watching unobserved the comings and goings from within the next-door house—a sprawling and ornate building that was now a private hotel. Ironwork chairs and tables, with sun-umbrellas, adorned the neatly mown lawn. There did not seem to be a swing there either, though there was a small bowling green and a badminton net.

The cat appeared, and sharpened its claws against the trunk of the tree with a rasping noise.

'What did you say your name was?' it said.

'Maria.'

'Mary, you mean.'

'No. Maria.'

'That's a bit fancy, isn't it?' said the cat scornfully.

'My mother thinks old-fashioned names are nice.'

'Pretentious, I call it,' said the cat. It watched a clump of grass intently, its tail twitching.

'Does the dog live next door?' said Maria. 'The one that barks in the night?'

The cat shuddered. 'Do you mind? One has some feelings.'

'I just wondered.'

Some children had come out into the hotel garden and were playing an energetic game of badminton, with much shrieking and shouting.

'Jolly lot,' said the cat. 'Why don't you ask if you can play with them?'

'I might.'

'Go on then.'

'In a minute.'

'You're scared they wouldn't want you,' said the cat.

Maria slid down the tree and walked slowly towards the ragged hedge that separated the two gardens at this point. The cat watched her through half-closed eyes. She stood looking at the children for a minute or so and then said, 'Actually, I've got to go in and help my mother.'

'Sez you,' said the cat.

In the kitchen, her mother was energetically filling shelves and cupboards with their kind of food, and sorting out the crockery.

'Why were you chasing that cat away?'

'It's an unfriendly cat,' said Maria.

'Nonsense. It's been purring round my legs all morning.'

Hasn't she ever noticed, Maria wondered to herself, that people can be quite different depending on whom they're with? Animals too, presumably. Like Mrs Hayward at school smiles and smiles when there are parents there so you see her teeth all the way round and then when there's only children again her face goes all long and thin and you don't see her teeth any more and her voice goes different too kind of quicker and crosser . . .

The front doorbell rang.

'A caller!' said Mrs Foster. 'But we don't know anyone.'

She went through to the hall. Beyond the open door Maria could hear the mixture of voices—a strange one and her mother's (that's her talking-to-people-she-doesn't-know voice, she thought). The voices ebbed and flowed; the kitchen clock ticked; the sun came out and made a neat golden square across half the table, down its legs and on to the floor. Maria became aware that she was being called, and went reluctantly into the hall.

'This is Maria,' said her mother. 'Mrs Shand is our landlady. She lives over the road.'

Mrs Shand was very old. Her clothes were old-fashioned but lady-like, Maria recognized; silk dress and brooches and necklaces, and stockings that ended oddly in a pair of white plimsolls. She stared at Maria and said, 'The last tenants had four. Just the one will be quite a change. Not that I mind children.'

I have never met a landlady before, thought Maria, so I don't know if I mind them or not. I expect I shall find out.

'Well,' said Mrs Shand, 'there's plenty of space for the three of you, that's for sure.'

'Plenty,' said Mrs Foster. 'We hadn't realized quite how large the house was.'

'Tenants are often surprised. The furnishings arouse comment also, from time to time.'

'We like Victorian things,' said Mrs Foster. 'Aren't you afraid of damage, though? With children about, and people being careless . . .'

'The house has been subjected to children all its life,' said Mrs Shand, a little tartly. 'I grew up in it myself, with six brothers and sisters. And my mother before me. It is too old to change, like me. I had the kitchen modernized, as they call it. People seemed to object to the old arrangements.'

Maria, who had been studying the face on a cameo brooch pinned to the neck of Mrs Shand's dress, and only half-listening to the conversation, began suddenly to pay attention. How very strange to be staying in a house in which a great many children had grown up. In her own home, there had only been her: it was built eight years ago, and was younger, in fact, that she was. She thought of Mrs Shand, standing in this same doorway years ago as a girl her own age. She stared at the landlady's face—hatched over with tiny, thread-like lines—for the shadow of this other person she must once have been, and could not find it. Had she, and others, leapt down those stairs three steps at a time, and sat in the tree in the garden?

'Maria,' said her mother, 'Mrs Shand was speaking to you.'

Maria jumped, and paid attention again.

'I asked,' said Mrs Shand, 'which room you chose for yourself.'

'The one at the back,' said Maria. 'The little one.'

'Ah. The old nursery. That was always the children's room. You can hear the sea at night.'

And the swing, thought Maria, and was going to ask about this swing when her mother began to speak. The conversation moved away to matters of newspaper deliveries and the electricity meter.

'Well,' said Mrs Shand, in a concluding tone of voice, 'I think that is about all I need to tell you. The piano was tuned last month. Please feel free to use it.' She looked reflectively at Maria. 'Quiet little thing, isn't she? You are welcome to call in if there is anything you wish to ask about.' And then her grey and white patterned silk back view vanished between the green hedges of the drive.

'She matches the house nicely,' said Mrs Foster.

'Why doesn't she live in it any more?'

18

'She finds it too big. She lives in a flat in the guest-house over the road.'

'I wish she'd taken her cat with her,' said Maria. And I wish I'd asked her about the swing, she thought. Never mind. Another time.

In the afternoon it rained. Excused the beach, Mrs Foster settled herself in the drawing-room to read, with barely concealed relief. Mr Foster went to sleep. Maria stared at the rain from her bedroom window for a while: it coursed down the glass in oily rivers, making the outline of the dark tree in the garden (her tree, as she now thought of it, the one that she had climbed that morning) swim and tremble like seaweed in a rock-pool. The thought of seaweed reminded her of the fossils from the beach and it occurred to her that she had meant to find out what they were called, and label them. She began to arrange them, comparing them with the ones in the miniature chest of drawers. Some were just the same, which made identification easy enough. She wrote their names in her best writing on small pieces of paper—*Promicroceras* . . . *Asteroceras* . . . —and arranged them in nests of cottonwool from the bathroom. It looked professional and scientific. One fossil, though, refused to be identified. It was a very ghostly thing, in the first place, just a hint of patterning on a lump of the blue rock that seemed at first glance to be nothing in particular. Only after a while did its lines and patterning become deliberate, the stony shadow of some ancient creature.

What I need, she thought, is a book. And downstairs in that room there are lots of books.

The books, though, when she stood among them in that library between the drawing-room and the dining-room, were quite remarkably unenticing. They reached from floor to ceiling in tiers of brown, maroon and navy blue. There was nothing gay in sight—not a coloured jacket or illustration—and when she pulled a book or two out at random they each had the same queer smell. It was the smell, she decided, of books that no one has got around to reading for a long time. And the gold-lettered titles on their spines were far from inviting: *The Origin of Species*, by Charles Darwin, *The Testament of the Rocks*, *The Principles of Geology*. It was as she stared at them with distaste, though, that it occurred to her that words like 'rock' and 'geology' were to do with fossils. She took one of the books down and there, sure enough, was a page of neat drawings of rock sections, and, a few pages later, of shells. The text, though, was as unintelligible, almost, as though it were in a foreign language, laden with cumbersome words that she could not understand and sentences so long that it was quite impossible to find out what they meant. The drawings, on the other hand, were nice, and one book at least looked as though it might be helpful. She selected an armful and took them upstairs to her bedroom.

Arranged in a row on the table they looked important, if daunting. She sat down at the table—an old, battered one it was, with inky grooves and at one side some deeply inked initials, H.J.P.—and opened *The Origin of Species,* not very hopefully. It was an extremely solemn book, though one page through which she skipped did talk quite interestingly about striped horses. Most of it she could not understand at all. She scowled at the book, scrubbing the heels of her sandals on the rung of the chair, while outside in the garden that small dog was barking again. This book isn't going to be any good, she thought, I don't really understand a word of it. She flipped through the pages, and as she did so the book fell open at the end, and there, on the blank last page, somebody had made drawings with a fine-nibbed pen, with writing beside each one.

Disapprovingly, because she had been brought up to believe that you should never scribble in books, Maria examined the writing, which she recognized as old-fashioned in its neat, sloping style, but a little uncertain, probably that of someone around her own age. There were several instances of mis-spelling. 'Specimins collected upon the cliffs' she read, and then there was a list of Latin names—*Gryphaea . . . Phylloceras . . .* (it was impossible, of course, to know

20

if these were correctly spelt or not)—with, beside each, a neatly penned drawing of a fossil. Several times the nib of the pen had caught on a rough bit of paper and spat a shower of minute ink dots which, in one place, the writer had turned into a little figure wearing a dress to below her knee, with a frilled pinafore on top, and black boots with many buttons. And long hair held back by a band. It was quite a good drawing. Better, thought Maria, than I could do. And then, running her eye down the page, she saw suddenly a drawing that looked familiar.

That's mine, she thought, that's the one I don't know the name of . . . And, laying her fossil beside the drawing, she saw its shadowy shape and patterning confirmed and defined in the tidy pen-strokes. *Stomechinus bigranularis*, said the writing alongside it, 'an extinct form of sea-urchin. Found below the west cliff, 3 August 1865.'

And it's August now, thought Maria, a different August . . . And with the book still open on the table in front of her she sat looking out of the window and thinking about someone else (a girl, I'm somehow sure she was a girl . . .) who had held the same book just about a hundred years ago—no, more than that—and looked perhaps out of the same window maybe at the same shaggy lawn and gently heaving trees. Because, thought Maria, I suppose she lived here, since the book is here, and the fossils in the cabinet, which must have been hers . . . And, thinking about this, and stroking her fingers over the smooth, but so faintly ridged, surface of the piece of grey rock containing *Stomechinus bigranularis*, she heard the squeak and whine of that apparently non-existent swing again.

Into which agreeable private dream intruded—as such things inevitably do—the voice of her mother calling that it was time for tea. But we've only just had lunch, thought Maria, I'm sure we have, it's not true at all that time is always the same, it simply isn't, there are slow afternoons and ordinary afternoons and afternoons like this one that are so fast they hardly seem to have happened . . . She went downstairs two steps at a time, jumping the last four in one leap, and noticed that the rain had stopped. She would be able to go and climb that tree again after tea.

The tree seemed, half an hour later, like an old friend. She settled herself in her armchair curve where branch met trunk. The bark was warmly rough against her back, through her cotton T-shirt, and the leaves hissed and whispered around her conversationally. After a while she was joined by a pair of pigeons who settled in another part of the tree and moaned at each other along a branch.

The sun had come out now and it was a bright, sparkling evening after the rain. The children from the hotel erupted into the next-door garden with much screaming and began to play badminton at the net not far beyond her tree. She made herself even smaller and more silent than she had been before, and watched them intently. There were three girls a little younger than herself, several smaller fry, and an older boy, who she assessed at, also, around eleven. She realized suddenly that they were the family she had seen at the petrol pump, on the way to Lyme—at least, given their ages and the number of them, they seemed to be a mixture of two families. The boy, she noticed, was slightly bored with the others. He played quite good-naturedly with the younger ones for a while, and then had an argument with the girls which sent him off on his own, kicking moodily at the stones around the edge of a flower-bed. Then, something in her tree attracted his attention and to her considerable alarm he came over and stood directly underneath it, staring up into the leaves. Maria froze against the trunk. The pigeons cooed at each other in monotonous repetition.

She must have clenched herself so tightly in her efforts to keep still that all of a sudden her sandal slipped against the bark with a rasping noise, the pigeons lumbered noisily off with cries of alarm and lurched down into another tree, and the boy, turning his head in her direction, looked straight up at her. They stared at each other through the leaves.

'I knew you were there all the time,' said the boy. 'I only pretended not to so I could watch the collared doves. What did you go and frighten them away for?'

'I didn't mean to,' said Maria.

He was examining the tree with interest now. 'That's a good tree,' he said. 'The ones in this garden are hopeless. Do you live in that house all the time?'

'No,' said Maria. She wanted, urgently, to share the tree with him, to invite him into it, but even as she started to do so the usual business happened, the process whereby she never, ever, in the end, said what she wanted to say, in case it was wrong, or the other person didn't want to do the thing suggested anyway, or would just stop listening. 'No,' she said.

'We came yesterday,' said the boy. 'They have rotten food. Not enough. But there's a colour telly, so I s'pose it's not too bad.' He put his hands in the pockets of his jeans, turning. He was about to go away.

'How did you know they were collared doves?' said Maria desperately.

'What do you mean?'

'Not pigeons. I thought they were pigeons.'

'Obviously they were collared doves, weren't they?' said the boy. 'I mean, wood pigeons have a wing bar, don't they? Anyway, the call's different.' He was wandering off now.

'Goodbye,' said Maria, her voice coming out suddenly loud, which made her go pink. Fortunately the leaves hid her.

''Bye,' said the boy. 'See you . . .' he added, casually. And then with a sudden whoop he was dashing over the grass to the rest of the children. Maria heard them shouting, 'Martin . . . Come on, Martin.'

Some time later she slid down the trunk of the tree and went back into the house. It was very silent. In the kitchen the fridge hummed softly. A clock ticked. Otherwise there was not a sound except for the rustle from the drawing-room when her father turned over a page of the newspaper. Her parents had adapted rapidly to the drawing-room. They sat on either side of the empty fireplace, in identical bulbous chairs, reading. Maria lay on her stomach on a darkly patterned rug, and read also. The cat arranged itself decoratively along the arm of a sofa and watched them.

'Lively holidays you people go in for,' it said.

'We're a quiet family,' said Maria.

It flexed its claws against the material of the sofa and said, 'Do anything stimulating today? Learn anything? Go anywhere? Have any interesting conversations?'

'I talked to quite a nice boy,' said Maria. 'He's about my age,' she added.

'Well, well,' said the cat, 'we are coming on, aren't we? I suppose he asked you to go over there and play.'

Maria did not reply.

'Well?' said the cat.

'Maria,' said Mrs Foster, looking up, 'don't mutter like that. And shoo that cat off the sofa, will you. It's ruining the material with its claws.' After a moment she added, 'You didn't need to chase it right out of the room, poor thing.'

'It wanted to go out,' said Maria. 'I think I'll go to bed now.'

She had a bath in the bath with feet like animals' claws. It was a particularly deep bath, so that once in it, lying down, you could not see out unless you sat up, and indeed, if as small as Maria, were in danger of drowning unless you kept constantly on the alert. Even so, she found it satisfactory. The lavatory, too, was pleasing. It had a brown wooden seat and a wreath of roses around the china basin, an arrangement she could not remember having come across before. Nothing in this house, she realized, was new. Everything was battered by time and use. In her own house, and those of all her friends, there were things that had been bought last month, or last year. In this one, wood was scratched, paint tattered, materials worn and faded. People had been here before. Such, for instance, as the H.J.P. who had carved her initials on the table. And the person—child,

24

girl?—who had made those drawings of fossils in the book from the library.

Going back to her room she realized also that this helpful, no-longer-here friend had told her the name of the one she had not been able to identify. *Stomechinus bigranularis* she wrote, neatly, on a piece of card. She arranged it with the rest of her small collection, got into bed and switched the light out.

3

Clocks and a Sampler

Pinned up on the kitchen wall—abandoned, presumably, by a previous tenant of the house, someone whose holiday was now over and done with—was a map of the town and the coast to right and left of it. Maria soon became very familiar with this map. She liked maps. She liked to know where she was and moreover had a deep secret pride in having learned all on her own how to find her way around a map. Once upon a time (and not so very long ago, either) maps had been as mysterious to her as the long columns of print in her father's newspaper, or some of the more confusing kind of sums at school, before which she sat in baffled horror. There were these maps, with their network of lines all differently coloured which might be roads or rivers or railways but you could never be certain which, and their blocks of green and blue and grey which meant other things, and their innumerable names. And there were the places to which they referred, bright and moving with houses and buses and waving trees and bustling people, and how on earth you married the one to the other, as it were, she could not see at all. How you stood before a map and said to yourself, ah! I am here, and I want to be there, so I must walk (or drive, or take a bus) in that direction. And then one day she had wrestled with this problem all on her own, standing in the shopping centre near her home before the street map that said so confidently, with its red pointing arrow, YOU ARE HERE. And all of a sudden she had realized where indeed she was, and the familiar streets and shops had turned themselves

26

into lines and writing and laid themselves handily out upon the map.

'Not very bright, were you?' said the cat. 'Most would have tumbled to that a long time ago.'

'I never said I was,' said Maria, 'bright.'

'Now take Sally in your class at school,' the cat went on, warming to the subject. 'She's what I'd call bright. Hand up all the time—"Please, miss, I know," "Please, miss, can I answer . . ." Nice writing. Red ticks all over her exercise books.'

But Maria found suddenly that she did not want to talk about Sally in her class at school. It was too nice a day—sun making a white glittering sheet out of the sea, the fields beyond the house ablaze with buttercups and daisies—and moreover, she wanted to look at the map undisturbed. The cat, ignored, went to squat on the kitchen doorstep, and Maria returned to the map. The beach to which they went, she knew, was at Charmouth, and the cliffs beyond it, between Charmouth and Lyme Regis, were called first Black Ven, and then Church Cliffs. And today, she knew, was the day to start exploring all this on her own, very slowly, at great length and in much detail and with conversations with anything likely that happened to come along.

They drove to Charmouth and walked along the beach, as they had done the first time they had gone there. To shake off the crowds, said Mrs Foster, and Maria thought, to get closer to Black Ven, and, thinking this, wondered why it should be called Black when in fact it was grey and green and golden. Picking their way along the beach she thought of this and other things while her mother selected and then discarded likely sitting-places with all the deliberation of someone buying a house. At last a place was found that was neither too windy nor too shady, neither too near the sea nor too far, un-encumbered by seaweed or noisy neighbours. Mrs Foster set about the process of making herself comfortable and establishing the boundaries of their territory, and Maria, watching her, thought that if you were a person who didn't know about seaside holidays—a visitor from outer space, say, or a prehistoric person—you might be amazed to find that at certain times of the year everybody gathers on the edges of England (and Scotland, and Wales) and just sits on them, looking at the sea. It might seem a very odd thing to do.

'All right?' said Mrs Foster.

'All right,' said Maria. And then, after a moment or two, 'I think I'll go and explore.'

'Mmn,' said Mrs Foster, opening her book.

Maria began to climb the slopes at the back of the beach, the toes of the cliff. Grey, muddy toes they were, and looking up she saw that this dried grey mud had slid in long tongues down from the top, like pictures of glaciers in geography books. The mud had cracked into scaly patterns, and here and there, as you walked upon it, it quaked a little as though deep down its foundations were uncertain. A notice back at the car park had warned sternly that these cliffs were dangerous and might fall at any time. And Maria, looking up at the blasted slopes of Black Ven, thought with a shudder, I'm not going up there, I don't fancy that at all.

For it was an eerie place. It seemed both very old and very young —old and infertile as the moon, with its barren reaches of mud and rock, and yet young as last week in its impermanence. For this, she saw, was the landscape of collapse. The cliffs had slipped and slid—sometimes long, long ago, so that the place that had crumbled away was now clothed in scrub, grass, reeds and sapling trees—and sometimes so recently that nothing yet grew at all except a few valiant seedlings poking out from the mud to show what they could do, given time and a world that would stop moving.

She followed a path that wound between bushes and over dried gullies lined with whispering reeds. It was a garden, this place, a wild garden over which the ashen cliffs presided like cathedral walls. There were flowers all around. Some of them she could recognize—the more ordinary ones. Vetch and ragwort and those little yellow things called eggs and bacon that are really birds' foot trefoil, and

28

clover. But there were plenty of others she did not know, including a most abundant green plant growing in forests like small pine trees, and something like a wild sweet-pea. She picked a piece of this and tucked it in her buttonhole, meaning to look it up in a book, if possible. She picked a dandelion head, and blew, babyishly, and it erupted into the wind in a shower of shiny fragments that drifted uselessly away towards the sea. Where, thought Maria, they haven't a hope of growing. Waste. You're always being told not to waste things—time and electricity and left-over food—but things waste themselves much more. All that growing and flowering and making seeds for nothing. Dandelions and those millions and millions of seeds from elm trees in the spring. And tadpoles. And all those ammonites that got fossilized in the rock, there must have been millions and millions of them, too. Seas full of them. All getting eaten by other things before they grew up. Talk about waste . . .

'What?'

She came round a large gorse bush to find herself face to face with someone who had been standing on the path, and realized with sudden shame that some at least of these thoughts had been said aloud. And the person, to make it worse, was the boy from the hotel next door.

'You've done it again,' he said. 'But I daresay you didn't mean to.'

'Done what?'

'Frightened the birds away. There was a pair of linnets.' He looked at her with mild irritation, which turned to active exasperation as something about her caught his attention. 'Where on earth did you get that?'

'What?'

'The grass vetchling,' said the boy crossly, 'stupid.'

Maria's hand flew to the now wilting flowers in her buttonhole. 'These? I didn't know what they were.'

'*Only* the rather rare grass vetchling,' said the boy, 'That's *all*. Don't you know this is a nature reserve?'

'No,' said Maria dolefully. The grass vetchling felt now as though it were burning a reproachful hole in her shirt.

He looked down at her—he was at least a head taller—and apparently relented a little for he said more tolerantly, 'Oh well, don't do it again, anyway,' and then, looking at her hand, 'can I see your fossil?'

It was a bit of ammonite, not very impressive, but all she had been able to find that morning. 'Super,' said the boy kindly. He fished in his pocket and brought out something that Maria recognized at once.

'*Stomechinus bigranularis,*' she said confidently.

The boy gaped in astonishment. 'Is that what it's called?' And then, 'How do you know?'

'There's a book in our house,' she said, after a moment 'About fossils.'

'What's your name?' said the boy briskly. It was clear that their relationship was getting on to a different footing.

'Maria.'

'Mine's Martin. Could I have a look at this book sometime?'

Maria glowed, and could do no more than nod.

'Ssh,' said Martin with sudden urgency, though she was standing perfectly still and silent. She followed his gaze to a small bird slipping from branch to branch of a bush. They watched it until it flew off.

'Stonechat.'

'Was it?' said Maria admiringly.

'Female. I say, what's the time?'

'Quarter past two.'

'I'll have to go back. We're going somewhere this afternoon. Come on.'

Maria followed him, although she had intended to continue with her exploration of the lower slopes of Black Ven. She walked behind him in silence, stopping obediently whenever he did, anxious to shed her reputation as a confirmed bird-frightener. Once, as they crossed

30

the bed of a gully over a plateau of dried and cracking mud, he said, 'It's dangerous here when there's been a lot of rain.'

'Why?'

'The cliff starts slipping. The water builds up on top, see, and then it all starts slipping and sliding down. Not usually in summer, though. February and March, mostly. This part can be all a kind of bog.'

'Do you come here always?'

'Most years.'

Down on the beach he said over his shoulder, casually ''Bye, then.'

''Bye.'

'I'll come and look at that book sometime, I expect.'

The rest of the afternoon seemed a little flat. Maria and her mother ate their sandwich tea. They read their books. Bravely, they bathed in a sea whose chill matched its stony colour. And as the sun began to sink in the sky Mrs Foster said, as Maria had known she would, 'Well, I think we've had the best of the day.'

Back at the house they found a note on the door-mat. Mrs Foster picked it up and they read, in large, loopy handwriting, 'It occurred to me that you might care to borrow a small handbook to places of interest to visit in the neighbourhood, which I happen to have. Perhaps the little girl would kindly call over this evening and I will give it to her.' It was signed, 'Hester Shand'.

'Our landlady,' said Mrs Foster. 'Would you mind, darling?'

Maria did mind, privately. She had not taken an instant liking to Mrs Shand; rather the opposite, indeed. But there was no good reason to refuse without making her mother cross, and she preferred not to have people cross with her. 'All right,' she said.

Mrs Shand lived in a large, much-turreted house called The Victoria Private Hotel over on the other side of the road. A notice at the entrance to the drive said 'No Turning'. A further one, halfway up, said 'Residents' Cars Only'. Small green signs warned you off the grass. There seemed to be much that was forbidden. A further notice beside the door of the hotel said flatly 'No Children or Dogs'. Maria stared at it, thinking it pointless. There are, after all, both children and dogs—lots of them, all over the place. So there's nothing to be done about it. You might as well say No Rain or Earthquakes. But what the notice meant, of course, was There Are To Be No Children Or Dogs Here. Which, Maria thought with a sudden rush of indignation, was rude. Nobody can help being a child or a dog, and indeed they're not bad things to be, one way and another. She was just about to ring the large brass bell beside the door when a small nameplate caught her eye, with another bell below it: Shand, Flat 1. Please Ring.

She rang. After about a minute a tube beside the bell, which she had not noticed, crackled and said 'Yes?', making her jump.

'My mother sent me to get the book.'

'Push the door,' said the tube breathily, 'and go up the stairs. The door at the far end of the landing. It is unlocked.'

The Victoria Private Hotel, within, was sunk in a deep (childless and dogless) silence. Maria climbed two flights of stairs, thickly carpeted, and found herself on a wide landing, confronted by many closed doors. The one at the far end did indeed have a further nameplate beside it saying Shand. She opened the door and went in.

Her first impression was that there was some kind of machinery at work. A small room, furnished only with a mirror and a marble-topped table, opened into another, larger one, and from the large one came a confusion of rhythmical noises, and, almost at once, Mrs Shand's voice saying, 'Please come through here.'

It was not machinery, but clocks. Mrs Shand sat on a large padded sofa (reminiscent of the ones in the drawing-room over the road) in the middle of a room otherwise furnished largely with clocks. There were other padded chairs, and small wobbly tables, and glass-fronted book-cases, and a very large fern in a pot, and many pictures, but the clocks dominated. They were mostly grandfather clocks, half a dozen of them at least, standing around the walls like so many tall,

32

insistent presences, ticking like an ill-assorted orchestra, all at odds with one another, some slow, some fast, some urgent, some with a halting note as though they would stop if only they could. She stared round at them in wonder, and they ticked at her in their different voices and at their different speeds, turning upon her their various faces. For they were all different. There were faces sternly simple and faces painted with flowers, a face ornately patterned in brass, a face above which a galleon rocked ceaselessly against a painted sea. Ten to two, said one, five to six, another—half past seven, twelve o'clock . . . The hands were all at odds. A muted argument about the time raged from one side of the room to another.

'The book is on the table,' said Mrs Shand. 'Please be careful. There are some valuable ornaments about.' She was working on a piece of embroidery. Gingerly, Maria approached a small, unsteady table (which lurched as she came near it) and took the book. Mrs Shand, over a needle she was threading, gave her a critical look.

'Of course,' she said, 'in my day a little girl would wear a frock. Nowadays all children wear trousers, so that for the life of me I cannot tell the difference. Not that it seems to matter any more. Enjoying your holidays?'

'Yes, thank you,' said Maria.

'There's nothing like the seaside, is there?'

Maria could think of no answer to this that would not lead the conversation into another dead end, so she said nothing. In any case it was clearly not a real question, for Mrs Shand had turned away to hunt for something in the sewing-basket beside her. Maria wondered if she might go now, but Mrs Shand suddenly said, re-emerging from the sewing-basket, 'I daresay you would like a chocolate.'

Maria was not, as it happened, particularly fond of chocolate, but could think of no way to refuse, so she said, 'Yes, please.'

'The silver box on the desk,' said Mrs Shand. 'The soft centres are on the right-hand side.'

33

There was a silence, invaded only by the ticking of the clocks, while Maria ate her chocolate (it tasted rather unpleasantly of violets) and Mrs Shand threaded her needle with a long length of pink silk.

'The clocks were my grandfather's collection. They will go to a museum when I die.'

This remark, also, was not one that could be followed up with any success. Maria finished her chocolate (with some relief) and said, 'How do you know what the right time is?'

'There is always the wireless.'

And there, indeed, it was, an up-to-date Japanese transistor, on a table beside the sofa.

'The clocks have not been altered since my grandfather's death. As a gesture of respect. He was a distinguished scientist.'

And in the time since then, presumably, they had run fast, or slow, or stopped and been re-wound, and thus ended in this state of fretful disagreement.

'The one beside the fireplace was the schoolroom clock, in the house you are staying in. It is not so valuable as some of the others, but attractive.'

It was indeed. The face was wreathed in painted flowers, which twined around the brass figures, and behind the brass hands, which said ten to four (it was in fact about six o'clock). Violets, clover, daisies, vetch: the flowers, in fact, of field and hedgerow. And beside each painted flower in tiny, sloping letters, was its name: Common Forget-me-not, *Myosotis arvensis*; Creeping St John's Wort, *Hypericum humifusum*; Woody Nightshade, *Solanum dulcamara* . . .

'Unfortunately it no longer works,' said Mrs Shand. 'The only one that is beyond repair, I am told. It broke down when my own mother was a child.'

At ten to four one day. Morning or afternoon? Maria wondered. Her attention shifted from the clock to a picture above the mantelpiece beside it. That, too, was interesting. It was an embroidered picture, not painted at all—a stitched house, with stitched writing above and below (she was too far away to read what it said), and small stitched objects, trees or animals or something, and a patterned border enclosing the whole.

'That is a Victorian sampler,' said Mrs Shand. 'Have a look at it. It is rather an unusual one. The little girl who made it would have been about your age, I should imagine.'

Maria stepped closer. The letters of the alphabet ran across the top of the sampler, and then the numbers one to ten. Below them was a row of creatures—a jolly prancing black dog, very small, and some things that might have been deer, and a couple of birds. Then there were some verses, which she read through.

> Think O my soul the solemn day
> Is sure and soon will come
> When I must quit this house of clay
> And hear my final doom
>
> Before the wise all-knowing god
> I quickly must be brought
> Who knows my evry way and word
> My evry secret thought
>
> His nature is all holiness
> Almighty is his powr
> How shall I stand before his face
> In that most solemn hour

Below that was a squarish red brick house, neatly sewn in cross-stitch. On one side of it were a pair of garden urns, the kind that you grow flowers in, and on the other a swing. It was a large and handsome swing, stitched in black, presumably to represent black iron-work. Underneath the house was a row of objects that Maria took at first to be flowers, since they were not unlike the formal flowers in the curly pattern that bordered the whole picture. Or they might have been snails. It was only after staring at them for a moment that she realized they were in fact fossils. Ammonites—small, spiral stitched ammonites. And below them, finishing off the picture, as it were, was a handsome and elaborately embroidered tree. There was lettering underneath the tree, more small black-stitched lettering: *Quercus ilex*, the holm oak. Finally, at the bottom, there was more lettering: Harriet Polstead aged 10 yrs her sampler. And then, below that: Susan Polstead completed this work for her sister 30 Sept 1865. Maria looked at it for a few moments in silence, and then said, 'She was younger than me, actually.'

'Possibly,' said Mrs Shand.

There was a further silence, while Maria studied the sampler and thought about this girl called Harriet, and then Mrs Shand said, 'Well, I daresay your mother will be wondering where you are.'

She looked expectantly at Maria and Maria said, 'I think I'd better be going now. Thank you very much for the book.'

'Not at all,' said Mrs Shand. And then, as Maria was almost out of the door, she added, almost sharply, 'I trust you're making good use of the piano.'

'Yes,' said Maria untruthfully.

'Quite right,' said Mrs Shand. 'Goodbye, then.'

Going back down the stairs of the hotel, so smugly shrouded in its child- and dog-rejecting silence (from somewhere on the ground floor came a discreet tinkle of tea-cups), Maria decided that she did not altogether care for Mrs Shand. Which was a pity because in fact there was a great deal that she would have liked to ask her about the clocks, and, even more, about the sampler. It was still in her head as she crossed over the road—its stiffly stitched flowers and that leaping black cross-stitch dog, and the swing and the urns and the plump cushiony shape of the tree at the bottom. *Quercus ilex*, the holm oak.

Because, she thought with a sudden gush of interest, that's my tree, I'm sure it is . . . It's the same shape, and the same very dark

36

green, and the same fat trunk and branches. And the house is the same house.

But there are no urns now, and no swing, and for some reason the house is a different colour. White, not brown.

She crossed the road and stood staring at the house. Behind and beyond it the sea made a grey backcloth flecked with white just as it must have done when it was built. That would always have been the same, that and the shape of the coast reaching away to right and left. And here was she, Maria, standing looking at it on an August evening just as the girl who made the sampler—what was her name, Harriet?—must have done once, a long time ago. Harriet is like the ammonites in the rock, she thought, not here any more but here in a ghostly way, because of the things she left behind. The sampler, and the drawings in the book. And it came to her, as she turned to go into the house, that places are like clocks. They've got all the time in them there's ever been, everything that's happened. They go on and on, with things that have happened hidden in them, if you can find them, like you find the fossils if you break the rock.

Before supper Mr Foster examined Mrs Shand's guidebook and made a neat list of Places of Interest to be visited during the course of the holiday, with map-references and a note about mileages. This filled Maria with a certain gloomy apprehension: she did not like this kind of arrangement, unavoidable as it was in a family like hers. Both her parents thought that it did you good to go and see interesting places. So Maria sat in silence while plans were made, and a discussion held about how many Dorset towns were Roman in origin.

'Well,' said Mr Foster, 'and what has Maria been doing?' He often referred to her as Maria when he was in fact speaking to her.

'I sat in the ilex tree,' said Maria.

'The what tree?' said Mrs Foster.

'The ilex tree. The one at the end of the garden.'

'Who told you it's called an ilex tree?' said Mr Foster.

Mr and Mrs Foster were town people: they tended to know a great deal about things that are discussed in the papers and on television, and to be good at finding the quickest way from one part of London to another, but not to know the names of things. Plants and trees and stars and that kind of thing. Maria had long observed that one of the many ways in which people are divided up into different kinds is the division between people who know the names of things, who usually live in the country, and people who do not, who usually live in towns. She herself was a town person, since she lived in a town, but thought that she was probably, secretly, inside, the other kind.

'Nobody, really,' said Maria. For some reason that she could not pin down, she found that she did not want to talk about the sampler. Probably they would not be interested, in any case. 'It's a kind of oak tree,' she added.

'No, it isn't,' said her father. 'Oak trees have acorns. And an entirely different leaf.' He spoke firmly and confidently: he was used to being right about things. It was always assumed, within the family, that he was right.

Maria said nothing. She looked at her father over the table and said nothing. He smiled affectionately at her as though to say that no one expected a person of eleven to be well-informed, and began to talk to his wife about matters arising from an article he had read in the newspaper, and presently Maria finished her supper and left the kitchen without either of them noticing. She was good at not being noticed. It was, she sometimes thought, the only thing she was good at.

She went out into the garden and lay on her stomach on the grass for a bit in the last warming rays of the sun. (The cat, purring with unctuous charm, came and lay beside her to begin with—'Oh, no you don't,' said Maria, 'I'm not talking to you this evening. You'll just spoil a nice day.' It stalked off in a huff, to roll destructively on the only flowers.) Presently, though, the sunlight ebbed away from the lawn and she wandered back into the house through the open french windows of the drawing-room.

It could never be a comfortable room, somehow, but it did now feel familiar. Even the huge dark pictures seemed to have been part of her life for much longer than two days. Though there were still things she had never noticed, like, for instance, the other glass dome on the table in that corner by the window, in which were two more stuffed birds (so faded that it was impossible to tell what their original colouring might have been). My friend, Maria told them, my friend Martin wouldn't approve of you being stuffed and put under a glass dome like that. And I quite agree. He knows all about birds and plants and what their names are and things like that but he didn't know the name of the fossil he'd found and I told him and he may be coming to look at the book about fossils. He said he would. I expect he will.

And like the silver-framed photographs on the mantelpiece, one of a whiskery man with a nice, benign face, the other of a group of people, grown-ups and several children, sitting under a tree in a garden. The ladies wore long dresses, and the children were much encumbered with bulky clothes and straw hats or bonnets. Everything was in shades of yellowish-brown. She examined them for a moment before moving over to the piano, with the thought—somewhat unenthusiastic—that she might play it.

Maria was only moderately good at playing the piano. She had had lessons since she was six and in fact quite enjoyed them. But she was not, she knew, good at it. Not like Julia next door at home, who was Grade VI and had won a competition. But it was a very splendid piano—a proper grand piano, not like the unobtrusive upright that fitted into the corner of the living-room at home. Sitting down at it, with the brown cover removed, she felt both swamped by it and somehow uplifted, as though one might indeed suddenly be able to place one's hands upon the keys and bring forth a fluent and silvery stream of music.

Which was not, of course, at all the case. She played through as much as she could remember of the piece she was learning at the moment, and it sounded much as it always did, jumpy with hesitations and wrong notes. She got off the piano stool and, lifting its lid, discovered within a pile of tattered and yellowing sheet-music. Most of the pieces were far too difficult. At the bottom, though, there was a thin leather-bound album, a collection of songs and tunes all bound together in a gold-tooled binding on which was stamped in gold lettering, S.C.P. 1860. One or two of these seemed more approachable to someone of her modest abilities, and she played them through, not worrying too much at her mistakes and enjoying the large, competent sound of the piano.

A movement, in the shadowy evening gloom of the room, distracted her and made her produce an ugly discord. The cat was squatting on the arm of a chair observing her.

'We aren't concentrating, are we? Not giving the matter our full attention. There's a certain basic lack of talent, too, I'd say.' It stared squint-eyed into the garden, its tail twitching slightly.

'You again,' said Maria. 'Thinking about eating the birds, I suppose.'

'That's always an interesting possibility,' said the cat.

'Beast.'

'Perfectly true. Of the species "cat", to be precise. *Felix felix*. So what's wrong with behaving like one?'

'Just because it's your instinct doesn't make it a *nice* way to behave. Sometimes I feel like hitting people and I suppose that's instinct but it's still a nasty thing to do,' said Maria.

The cat curled up like a bun and closed its eyes. 'My, we are feeling argumentative this evening, aren't we?'

'In fact,' Maria went on, 'when I come to think about it I suppose that's the difference between us. That I try not to do things that might be nasty even if they are my instinct and you just don't bother. In fact you don't know what nasty is.'

'Oh, clever clever,' said the cat irritably.

'And the other thing, of course, that's different is that you can't remember things like I can. What did we have for lunch yesterday?'

'Don't pester me with details,' said the cat.

'There you are! And of course the most important thing is that you can't talk. Unless I let you.'

'Oh, shut up,' said the cat. It slid off the arm of the chair and made a sinuous exit into the garden, without looking at her.

And the other thing, of course, Maria thought, is that it can't expect things either. Like wondering what we're going to do tomorrow and if it'll be good or bad, and thinking how funny that I don't know now—anything might happen, there might be the end of the world, or an earthquake, and I simply don't know but by this time tomorrow I will. She put the music away and closed the lid of the piano.

Lingering over this odd thought, and with it other confused but not really unpleasant thoughts—of that sampler, of fossils, of Martin —she went upstairs to her room, undressed, washed, and was lying tidily in bed when her parents called in, singly, to say goodnight. Mrs Foster adjusted the bedclothes, removed some dirty socks and a shirt, and said, looking out of the window, that there was a lovely sunset and she thought that meant good weather.

'Not an earthquake, then,' said Maria, from deep within the bed, mostly to herself.

'What, dear?'

'Nothing.'

'Well, goodnight, then.'

'Goodnight.'

Her father came in and gave her one kiss with exactly the same careful deliberation that he gave her twenty pence pocket money every Saturday morning. This did not, Maria had worked out, mean that he did not love her but just that he believed money to be important. He always knew exactly how much money he had, or should have, in his pocket, in just the same way that he always cleaned his shoes at the same time every evening and always folded the newspaper right side out before throwing it in the dustbin. He was a very tidy person. I am tidy too, thought Maria, I suppose I have inherited tidiness like I have inherited my mother's straight hair, but I am untidy in my head, in the things I think about . . . And, thinking this, and wondering if, were it possible—and oh, how amazing and interesting it would be if it were—to somehow arrive within someone else's head and listen to thoughts as though to the radio, other people's would be as perplexed and as peculiar as her own, she sank gradually into sleep.

And heard, she thought, though by the morning she hardly remembered having done so, the distant sound of the piano being played. The very song she had tried to play herself, but more competently managed.

4

The Cobb and Some Dinosaurs

'What would you like to do?' said Mrs Foster. 'Beach? Or something different?'

'Something different.'

'What?'

'I don't know,' said Maria. They looked at each other, a little disagreeably, across the breakfast table. Mrs Foster thought that Maria was being unhelpful; Maria thought that her mother should have some interesting alternative already worked out.

'In that case,' said Mrs Foster, 'you can come down into the town with me, to the library. And then we could go for a walk along the Cobb.'

'The what?'

'The Cobb is the harbour wall. You can walk along it. It's very old. I daresay,' Mrs Foster added without enthusiasm, 'you could buy an ice-cream or something at the end of it.'

Maria stared at her mother coldly. She was not in fact thinking of either ice-cream or the prospect of walking along the harbour wall, and she did not mean to look cold. It had occurred to her that she had a reason for wanting to go to a library herself: the cool expression was simply what happened to her small, rather pale face when she was deep in thought. It frequently gave rise to misunderstandings.

'And there's no need to look so cross about it,' said Mrs Foster.

Coming out of the drive Maria noticed for the first time that the house had a name. It was a well-concealed name, the letters being simply cut into the white plaster of the two columns at either side of the drive gates but not picked out in any way, so that they were white against a white background: Ilex House.

They descended the steep streets that led down into the town. When places are clothed in tarmac, houses, walls, shops and lamp-posts it is difficult to remember that beneath lies earth, rock and the natural shape of the land. In the heart of London, in Oxford Street, Maria had been startled once to see workmen lift a slab of paving to reveal, beneath, brown earth. It was as though the new, shrill street of concrete and plate-glass windows had shown its secret roots. But here, she noticed, in this small seaside town, the roots came boldly out on to the surface, for walls and the occasional house were made of the same grey-blue stone as the cliffs. It seemed, somehow, satis-factory, as though the houses had grown out of the soil just like the trees and grass and bushes, settling down to match the pewter sky and the pale green sea below it. And as they passed a terrace of cottages she saw suddenly the coiled glint of an ammonite, enshrined there for ever in the wall beside a net-curtained window in which stood a vase of plastic flowers.

They arrived at the library, and Mrs Foster became involved in the complicated process of acquiring temporary tickets. Maria left her and began to search for what she wanted. It did not take very long: libraries are obliging places once you have got the hang of them. 'Trees', she soon discovered, came under 'Botany', and here was a fat book, lavishly illustrated with trees in all sizes and shapes. She found what she wanted and sat reading with quiet satisfaction; '*Quercus ilex*, the holm oak—common in gardens and parks, this handsome tree with dark, evergreen foliage and brownish-black, deeply fissured bark was introduced from Southern Europe during the sixteenth century . . .'

Her mother's face appeared at her shoulder. 'What are you reading?'

44

Maria indicated, in silence.

'Oh,' said Mrs Foster. 'That tree you were talking about . . .' Then, after a moment she added, 'Actually you were right. It does seem to be a kind of oak tree.'

Maria said nothing. She closed the book and put it carefully back on the shelf, patting it into line with its neighbours.

'Yes,' said Mrs Foster, after a brief silence during which she looked rather oddly at her daughter. 'Well, I suppose he was wrong, as it happens.' She seemed about to say something else, and then stopped.

They walked out of the library in silence, books tucked neatly under their arms, and down the steps into the street. As they turned towards the harbour Mrs Foster said, 'Of course, living in a town all the time that's the kind of thing you never really know much about. One tree seems much like another.'

'Not really,' said Maria.

Her mother looked mildly surprised. 'Well, I suppose not, when you look.'

After a moment she went on, 'Do you do about plants and things at school?' She sounded quite respectful, as though, Maria thought, she were talking to someone important, not me at all.

'Not very much,' said Maria. She thought of plants at school— beans in jam-jars with blotting-paper that got all smelly and enormous white roots twining round and round inside the jar. And mustard and cress on bits of flannel. But what I like, she thought, is not all that but the names of things. And every single kind of thing having a different name. Holm oak and turkey oak and the sessile and pedunculate oak. Sessile and pedunculate . . .

'What?' said Mrs Foster.

'Nothing.'

They had now reached the little harbour. The boats there were of a scale to match it—dinghies and rowing boats dapper in new coats of white paint, their names brisk in black or blue; *My Lady, Chopper II, Jester*. There was a smell of tar, petrol, and fish. The boats rocked gently on sheltered water that glinted here and there with rainbows of oil: beyond, on the seaward side of the Cobb, the waves sucked and lashed at the stone, and the green water was marbled with foam. The curving stone barrier along which they now walked seemed to divide two worlds. In the cosy, ordered world of the harbour each boat had its circle of admirers, grooming, coiling ropes; white sea-gulls screamed over pickings of orange peel, crusts, tea-leaves. Beyond the protection of the Cobb, the sea behaved as it liked, and there the gulls seemed both wilder and more competent, rocking with folded wings from one wave to another, or sailing effortlessly on the wind, their hard and staring eyes sometimes level with Maria's as they swooped low in passing. She wondered if one kind of gull settled for the squabbling life of the harbour, while others chose to rough it on the open sea, or if all gulls did both, or what. And then there seemed to be a third, inland way of life, for looking up at the patch-work of fields running back beyond the town, she could see more gulls scattered behind a ploughing tractor. Presumably, in fact, the cleverest gulls tried everything and then continued with whichever place provided most food, and so became the fattest and strongest gulls also . . .

But I'd choose the sea, she thought, if I were them. Not apple cores or muddy worms. Real fish, even if you hardly ever caught one.

They reached the end of the Cobb. 'I'm sorry,' said Mrs Foster, 'there don't seem to be any ice-creams.'

'I don't want one,' said Maria. And she didn't. It was quite enough to sit on the edge of the stone, with her legs hanging down over the water, looking across the harbour at the town. She could see their house, half hidden among trees, to the left, and then to the right the main part of the town spilling down between hillsides to a sea-front of ice-cream coloured cottages, green and pink, and a pale edging of sand before the sea began. It was a lovely day. Not, Maria thought, a straightforward lovely day with a boring blue sky and

46

nothing in it but the sun, but better than that because the sky was pleasantly busy with clouds, huge shining heaps of cloud that roamed across the horizon, ebbed and flowed, formed and reformed as you watched them. And every now and then they blotted out the sun for a few minutes, so that bands of sunshine fled along the coastline, spread out before her here in a huge receding curve. Everything would go grey and muted, as the sun went in, and there would be this band of golden colour sweeping along the cliffs to Weymouth, lighting up now a bright slice of rock, now a green field, now the white sparkle of a house, now the turquoise of the sea itself.

'What are you looking at, Maria?'

'Nothing,' said Maria. Then she added, 'Just the sun,' because that sounded rude, as well as being untrue.

'Nice day,' said her mother.

Mrs Foster took some postcards out of her handbag and began to write on them. First she addressed them (to Aunt Ruth, the neighbours, grandfather, and her friend Elizabeth), and then she wrote the messages. The messages, Maria could see, were all nearly the same. They said that we were having good weather, Lyme was pleasantly unspoilt and the rented house very nice.

When I'm grown-up, thought Maria—if I ever do grow up, which isn't something you can ever imagine actually happening—when I'm grown-up I shall come back here and think of myself sitting here now, today. And having thought this, in an off-hand sort of way, the thought suddenly took shape, most startlingly, so that a grown-up Maria (wearing spectacles, for some reason, with a handbag tucked under her arm, and dressed in a tweed suit like Aunt Ruth's) stood before her, smiling quite benevolently, and so real that it seemed almost possible that other people might see her also.

'Please let me introduce you to my mother,' said Maria, 'I mean to your mother.'

'Maria, you're muttering again,' said Mrs Foster, looking up from the postcards, 'It's getting to be a habit. You really must stop.' Maria

47

said guiltily, 'Sorry,' and the grown-up Maria smiled once more and dissolved most gracefully into the sea. Which, Maria felt, was the best place for her, because harmless as she appeared the thought of her was somehow entirely unwelcome. I don't want to be like that, thought Maria comfortably, I want to be me as I am now for ever and ever.

A boat was arriving at the end of the Cobb—a very nautical-looking boat sprucely painted in pale blue and white, with much rope and sail displayed, but that nevertheless ran on a noisily chugging engine that now spluttered to a stop as it reached the steps. A party of people got off, children and adults. They were on the Cobb before Maria realized that it was Martin and his family.

They approached, an untidy and vociferous party, the grown-ups talking loudly, the younger children clamouring and arguing. Martin trailed behind, looking, she thought, bad-tempered. He wore jeans with holes in both knees, and a jersey tied around his waist.

He saw her. 'Hello.'

'Hello.' Maria shot a wary glance at her mother, who looked up from the postcards.

'They're a rotten cheat, those boats,' said Martin. 'Fifty pence and all you get is ten minutes pottering about round the harbour. I think they're frightened of the real sea.'

The rest of his family had sat down a few yards away, locked in argument about which beach they should go to. Mrs Foster, looking uneasy, said, 'Oh, are they?' Children often had this effect on her parents, Maria had noticed—strange children. Boys especially.

'Have you been?' said Martin to Maria. 'I shouldn't bother.'

It now dawned on Mrs Foster that Maria and Martin knew one another. 'You're in the guest-house next door to us?' she said.

Martin nodded. There was a silence, awkward only for Mrs Foster, who clearly could think of nothing else to say, and Maria, who yearned to, but was as usual throttled into silence by her feelings. Martin was absorbedly picking at a limpet exposed by the ebbing tide. 'Can I come over and have a look at that book tonight?' he said suddenly.

They were now all three engulfed by the rest of Martin's family, younger children, older children, and two women—one, it became apparent in a confusion of explanations and remarks, being his mother and the other his aunt. The children divided fairly evenly into two families of cousins. It seemed, to Maria, like being suddenly in the middle of a flock of starlings. She saw her mother furtively gather her possessions around her, as though they might be trodden on, or removed. Martin's mother had launched straight into an impassioned account, much punctuated with laughter, of a visit to Weymouth they had made the day before. Impressively, she was able to talk uninterrupted while at the same time preventing one small child from falling into the sea and re-dressing another. Mrs Foster listened with a rather fixed smile: they were not, Maria could see, at all the same kind of person.

'. . . So we decided you can keep your classy resort,' concluded Martin's mother. 'In future we're stopping here.' Her attention strayed to Maria as she finished buttoning someone's trousers. 'Are you on your own? You must come over and play with the girls.'

'That would be nice, wouldn't it?' said Mrs Foster doubtfully.

'Any old time. Well, come along then, all. Martin?'

'I'll stay here for a bit.'

'All right. Get back in time for lunch, though. And don't be a nuisance to Mrs . . . er . . .?'

'Foster,' said Maria's mother.

'We're Lucases. Both lots. Well, 'bye for now, then.' They trailed off along the Cobb, audible long after they were out of sight behind a building.

Mrs Foster looked apprehensively at Martin. She did not much like boys. Maria always felt that one of the few things she had done right in her life was to be a girl.

'I thought I'd go to the museum,' said Martin.

Mrs Foster brightened. She had obviously expected something much more destructive or energetic.

'What a good idea. Maria hasn't been there either.'

They walked slowly back to the town. Martin explained to Mrs Foster, lengthily and patiently, how an outboard motor works. Mrs Foster said 'Yes,' and 'I see,' at intervals. Maria, happy, trotted two steps behind. It seemed to be quite all right for her to say nothing. At the entrance to the museum Martin said to her, 'Actually, your mum didn't follow all that,' and she said wisely, 'No, I don't think she did.'

Inside the museum Mrs Foster said, 'I'm afraid it looks a bit dull.' She began to move dutifully from glass case to glass case, spending the same length of time at each. Maria had seen her use the same system on picture exhibitions.

The cases were full of fossils. Fossils of a much greater variety and perfection than any one could imagine finding for oneself. Ammonites as big as door-knockers; chunks of rock through which swam the bony tracery of complete fish; the vertebrae of dinosaurs; the imprint of reptilean feet on a slab of clay . . . And the labels describing each item battered the reader with immensities of time—forty million years ago, a hundred and eighty million, four hundred million. Here were creatures younger by hundreds of millions of years than others. And here were charts that explained, with helpful drawings of rampant dinosaurs, fish of the most weird and impractical design, and all the smaller fry by way of shells and starfish and things that creep or crawl, which creatures had lasted for how long. Ammonites, Maria noted with surprise, were a relatively late invention, sharing a swampy and tropical universe with diplodocus and pterodactyl.

And all these creatures, she saw, studying charts and pictures, have stepped out of the rock of which the place is made, the bones of it, those blue cliffs with which England ends.

'Blue lias,' said Maria.

'What?'

'It's called blue lias, the rock here.' And she said it again, to herself, because she liked the sound of it. Blue lias . . . And the brown rock on top of it is called upper greensand, and all these different kinds of rock are different ages, like the fossils, old and older and very old indeed. They lie, sleeping, as it were, under fields and towns, full of the shells and bones of creatures that once were here.

'Good, isn't it?' said Martin. He pored over the cases, scowling in concentration.

Everything changes. The earth's surface heaves and boils: seas become land, continents are swallowed up by water, mountains are flung up. And through all this marches an endless procession of life-forms, from the unambitious shell-like creatures of this case, to the lumbering dinosaur of that picture. (Why, Maria wondered, reading the caption, should it matter so much that its brain was only the size of a kitten's? . . . Kittens manage, after all.) One thing gives way to another, and eventually all ends up, as the chart indicated at the bottom, on a note of undisguised triumph, with naked but bearded man, standing arms akimbo on what appeared to be Dover cliffs.

'Noah's Ark isn't true at all,' said Maria, with sudden illumination.

''Course not,' said Martin. 'It's a load of old rubbish.'

'Then people should say so,' said Maria crossly. She felt cheated. All your life you accepted blithely one account of things, and then you found yourself presented with something entirely different (and much more appealing). It needed thinking about.

They were moving together from case to case now. Occasionally Martin would give her an amiable poke to attract her attention . . . 'Look at that . . . Hey, come here . . .'

'It's as though,' said Maria, 'somebody was messing about with it all. Trying to see what would work and throwing away the things that didn't.'

'No, it isn't. It's evolution. We did it at school. Things change themselves—or bits of themselves—so that they fit in with where they're living. They grow longer legs or stop having tails or learn to eat something different. And the things that don't just die out.'

'I see,' said Maria reflectively.

Mrs Foster had reached the exit now, having completed her tour. They could see her, from the gallery on which they now were, sitting down to wait for them, opening her newspaper.

A large chart entitled *The Descent of Man* demonstrated this in the form of a tree from whose branches burst forth one creature after another, flourishes of Alice-in-Wonderland invention whose basic wrongness became apparent as their particular branch came to an abrupt end with some bizarre and extinct animal. At the top of the tree, having scrambled triumphantly up through mammals and apes, stood naked and hairy man again.

'It's like snakes and ladders,' said Maria. 'Throw a six and you stand on your hind legs.'

Martin gave her a look of guarded approval. 'Except that they didn't know they were doing it. Each bit took millions of years.'

'We must be too. Changing.'

'I'll grow two more arms. Better for climbing trees. And a tail.'

'That's going backwards again. I want eyes at the back as well as at the front.'

'Two mouths. So you could eat first and second course both at once.'

'Legs that expanded, like a music-stand. So you could run faster when you need to.'

They began to giggle. Mrs Foster, down below, looked up in surprise.

'We are, though,' said Maria. 'Seriously, I mean, changing all the time. Growing up. Getting taller and growing new teeth.'

'That's different.'

'More peculiar,' said Maria, 'because you know it's happening.'

But Martin had lost interest. He was examining the postcards at the exit. They each bought two rather muted postcards of fossils

('Wouldn't you rather have a nice view?' said Mrs Foster. 'Or one of the beach?'), and then set off on the climb up through the town back to the house. It seemed a very much shorter walk than it had ever done before. Disconcertingly soon they were outside the drive gates and Martin was saying, 'Well, 'bye then . . .' and, politely, 'thank you for having me.'

Lying in bed that night, waiting for sleep, Maria floated back in her mind to the night before. Same bed, same window, same curtains. But between them twenty-four hours of time during which things had happened. Nothing in particular (except that I had a nice time with Martin at that museum) but time none the less, which changes everything. Even, she thought, me. I'm not the same as I was last night. Not absolutely exactly the same. I *look* the same—except that I suppose I'm just a very tiny bit bigger, because I must have grown —but I'm not the same, not quite the same, because I've seen things and done things and thought things I hadn't this time yesterday.

Downstairs, her mother's voice came up in fragmented clips of a conversation with her father '. . . not at all a tiresome boy, really . . . fascinated by the museum, for some reason . . . positively chattering, she was . . .'

And I might, Maria thought, falling away into sleep, I just might tell Martin sometime about that sampler, and the clocks, because he might think they're interesting too. But I'm not sure yet. I'll have to think about that.

5

The Day that was Almost Entirely Different

'*Gryphaea*,' said Martin. 'It's a Mesozoic oyster.'

'I wonder what they were like to eat?'

'O.K. for ichthyosauruses, presumably,' said Martin, 'with a nice piece of toast.'

Gryphaea was a kind of fossil that the beach provided in abundance, curled grey stones like snails. They had five of them now.

'What we need,' said Martin 'is a brontosaurus vertebra. Some hope.'

They were examining the books in the library. In the hall, Mrs Foster passed once or twice, looking into the room as she did so. Martin's presence unnerved her: she expected him to break something.

'Why don't you go and play outside, you two?'

'We're just going to,' said Martin blandly. He was very good with grown-ups, Maria could see, in a way that she was not. It usually ended up with them doing what he wanted, rather than the other way around. Mrs Foster went into the kitchen and closed the door.

'James nicked my *Stomechinus* yesterday. I found it, though. And I belted him—not hard—and he told Mum and I got sent to bed early.'

James, Maria thought, was brother, not cousin. About four. It was hard to be sure, though—she never could sort them all out. She nodded sympathetically.

'You can't win,' said Martin with sudden gloom, 'when you're the eldest. Whatever you do, you shouldn't have because you're old enough to know better. And you spend your life fetching things from upstairs. Other people's jerseys. Look—there's a fantastic fossil! S'pose we found one of those!' They had come across a book with particularly clear and satisfactory illustrations.

'We won't.'

'We might.'

'We can't. It comes out of the wrong kind of rock. It's a trilobite, and you only get them in much older rock than the kind we've got here—blue lias. They were extinct by the time our kind of rock was made.'

'Pity,' said Martin. 'They could roll up like woodlice, it says here. Oh, well . . . You know something?' he went on, looking at Maria with a dissecting stare, as though he had her at the far end of a powerful microscope.

'What?'

'You're the only girl I've ever come across who wasn't like some-body's sister. Mine, for instance. I daresay it's because you aren't. Anyone's sister.'

There are some supremely agreeable moments in life that are best savoured alone—the first barefoot step into a cold sea, the reading of certain books, the revelation that it has snowed in the night, waking on one's birthday . . . And others the full wonder of which can only be achieved if someone else is there to observe. Such, Maria thought sadly, as this. For having said it, Martin had already turned away to explore the rest of the room. No one else would ever know.

'It's a pretty weird house, this.'

'It's all Victorian. The real thing, my mother says.'

'Better than a rotten old hotel.'

'The lady it belongs to lives over the road,' said Maria. 'She's got lots of clocks. And a queer picture—a sewn picture, not a painted one. The girl who made it was about the same age as me.'

55

'How do you know?'

'It says so. And when she made it. 1865. I keep thinking about her. I keep wondering what happened to her.'

'She grew up, didn't she?' said Martin briskly. 'She grew up and got married and had children and all that stuff. I say, there's a super atlas here.'

There was a silence. Martin pulled the atlas out and flipped over the pages.

'I don't feel as if she did,' said Maria at last. 'I feel as though she's still here, somehow.' She added, in a voice which was meant to be defiant but which came out merely as quiet, 'The same age as me.'

'That's daft,' said Martin. 'She isn't, is she? Unless you think she's a ghost or something. And that would be even more daft.' He hoisted the atlas back on to the shelf. 'Fact is, she's dead. Ages ago.'

'I s'pose so,' said Maria coldly.

'Stands to reason. Come on, let's go.'

Later that evening she went and sat alone in the ilex tree, after Martin had gone back to his family. It was a very soothing tree. Not just a good, private place in which to be, but somehow enclosing and companionable with its warm rough bark and its whispering, shifting leaves, darker and more leathery than the leaves of ordinary trees. Sitting in it, back against the trunk, legs stretched out along a fat branch, everything swayed and moved around you and yet at the same time you seemed to feel the roots of the tree reaching down, down into the ground, tethering it so firmly that it must be solid as a house, immovable. It had been making acorns, the tree; there were green berries in their scaly cups all around her, pale against the dark shiny leaves, hundreds of them. They wouldn't, of course, make hundreds of trees. None, probably. Waste, again. Sleepily, Maria watched the shadow of the tree get longer and thinner across the lawn, and told it about her day. We fossil-hunted, she said to it, down on the beach, my friend and I, my friend Martin, that is—

56

but of course you know about him because he's climbed you too—
and we found another *Gryphaea* and a bit of a *Stomechinus* but not
a very good one, and tomorrow I'm going out for the day with
Martin's family. I'm invited. Actually, she said to the tree, I'm not
all that sure about that. There's so many of them, and they all talk
at once. It makes me nervous. But I think I want to go.

'Remember to say thank you for having me.'
'Yes.'
'You've got your comb in your pocket?'
'Yes.'
'If you feel sick in the car, tell Mrs Lucas.'
No, thought Maria. In front of them all? Do you really think I
would? Die, quietly, just like that, is what you'd have to do.
'Have a lovely day.'
Over at the hotel (having had to wait, alone and conspicuous,
pink to the roots of the hair, in the hall until noticed) she found that
the Lucas families were neither ready nor decided about what they
were going to do. For the next half-hour there was a fever of dressing
children, sending Martin to find other children who had strayed
away somewhere, looking for things that had got lost, and arguing
about where they should go. Two girls jumped up and down, without stopping for an instant, shouting, 'We want to go to the fun-
fair! We want to go to the fun-fair!' Above this Martin's mother
administrated.
'What do you mean, you haven't *got* a dry T-shirt? There must be
one. Then wear one of Jane's.'
I've never worn somebody else's clothes, thought Maria. That's
one of the lots of things I haven't ever done in my life. A picture of
her own clothes came before her eyes, laid out clean on the chair at
the end of her bed every night ready for the next morning, the dirty
ones taken away to be washed.

57

'There's stock-car racing at Beaminster,' said Martin. He had said it three times already, but without much conviction, as though aware that it was a hopeless case.

'We want to go to the fun-fair!'

'Then look under the bed for them. James—come here!'

'Beach! Beach, *beach,* BEACH!'

'Susie, do your hair.'

'Fun-fair!'

'BEACH!'

'I can't find my shoes.'

'Do your hair.'

'FUN-FAIR!'

'Go and wash your face.'

'BEACH!'

'No, you can't have a lolly now.'

'I can't find my shoes.'

'Oh . . . SUGAR . . .' said Martin in sudden rage. He went and stood staring morosely into the garden.

'I think,' said Martin's aunt, 'that the visitor should be allowed to choose. What would you like to do, Maria?'

'BEACH!'

'FUN-FAIR! FUN-FAIR! FUN-FAIR!'

'All right. That's enough. Leave her alone,' said Mrs Lucas. 'James, don't keep pulling her jersey like that.' From under a heap of dirty nappies, toys, and wet bathing things she pulled a local newspaper. 'Blandford Forum Gymkhana—God, no! Flower Show at Child Okeford—not with this lot, thank you very much. Motor Cycle Scramble . . .' ('Yes, great, let's get going then . . .' said Martin, but in the tones of one who knows there is no hope.) '. . . Horse Show, Pottery Exhibition . . . Here, what about this, then? "Medieval Fayre. Spent a day in the fifteenth century at lovely Kingston Peverell Manor . . . Jousting, Archery, Ox-roast, Medieval Banquet, Minstrels. And many other attractions, including Produce

58

Stall and Teas. Entrance 25p. By kind permission of Sir John and Lady Hope-Peverell." How about that?'

'Can we joust?'

'I want an ox.'

'Oh, no,' said Martin wearily, 'not a stately home . . .'

Maria knew what he meant. She was herself something of an expert on stately homes. Mr and Mrs Foster enjoyed a drive to such places on a Sunday afternoon: it got you out of London, you saw the countryside (conveniently displayed, neither muddy nor cold, on the other side of the car windows) and you were taking an interest in history. Such outings could do you nothing but good. Maria had trundled obediently, at one time or another, up the stairs and through the rooms of Knole, Woburn, Blenheim, Hampton Court, Longleat and many another. Sometimes there were lions or dolphins, and sometimes there were not. When there were such additions to what was already on offer, the history part seemed to have been put rather firmly in its place, as though the owners were faintly apologetic about it, being quite well aware that not everyone cares for that kind of thing and not wanting to press the point. Indeed you were obviously free to give it a miss altogether if you preferred. The Fosters, though, did not. They would join conducted tours of the stately home in question, and Mr Foster would occasionally ask questions of the guide about a picture, or suit of armour. Maria found this intensely embarrassing.

'*Not* a bloody stately home,' said Martin.

'Martin! Don't be silly, anyway—it's obviously a special do, this. Right, that's settled then. Jerseys. Anoraks. Everybody have a pee before we go.'

Hours later, it seemed, in the car, wedged between someone's thigh and someone else's elbow, Maria again watched Dorset unfurl at either side of her—fields, hills, villages. Everybody talked at once, and pointed things out. As a journey, it bore as little relation to journeys with her parents, in the hushed interior of their carefully cleaned car, as the Underground in rush-hour to a First Class train compartment. This car was, within, ankle-deep in sweet-wrappers and iced lolly sticks, and without, coated in dust on which Martin had written various rude comments about its condition. It came as something of a relief to reach their destination after twenty minutes or so. A small queue of cars was moving slowly into a field car park. A banner, slung across the entrance to the stately home, said 'August Fayre', in huge but distinctly amateurish red letters (it had once, Maria could see, been a bedspread). The house, as such things went, was not at all stately. Not, admittedly, the kind of place one lived in oneself, but certainly not in the Woburn/Blenheim/Longleat league. Old, evidently, and with all those external bits and pieces like stone mushrooms and stone balls on the tops of pillars, and wrought-iron gates, that imply grandeur, but with other, more homely touches such as a forgotten dustbin lid beside the entrance, and an abundance of weeds in the flower-beds. There were large numbers of people about, and a distant, cheerful, jangle of music.

They spilled out of the car. 'You big ones can get lost,' said Mrs Lucas briskly. 'Twenty pence each and see you at half past four, back here.'

The big ones, it seemed, included also Martin's sister and girl-cousin. Ten yards from the car park he did a quick deal with them which involved giving them two pence each out of his twenty in exchange for which they were to keep away.

'I'm not being lumbered with them all day,' he explained. 'Anyway they're only nine.'

'Most people think I'm nine,' said Maria, 'because of being small.'

'Well, you aren't, are you? It's what people are that matters, not what they look like. Come on.'

Maria, weaving through the crowds behind him, wished that she was able to say exactly what she meant like that. Out loud, not just to cats and trees and petrol pumps. There seemed to be no difficulties about being Martin: he just *was*, like some kind of business-like, confident dog. Though, she now saw, he was not as good as managing his own mother as he was at managing other people's. But it is, of course, nearly always the case that other people's grown-ups are more persuadable than one's own.

It was extremely odd, this Fayre. All the people officially involved with it in one way or another, from the cark park attendant to the ladies running the produce stalls or the tea tent, wore historical clothes. From which particular bit of history did not seem much to matter—there were assorted long dresses, some topped with vaguely medieval head-dresses, one or two hairy dressing-gowns, hitched round the middle with rope ('I'm a friar,' explained the car park attendant kindly, 'in case you were wondering. Not what I'd choose as a get-up, myself, but we all got to do our bit.'), sundry shepherd-esses and milkmaids, and a great many muscular legs stuffed into tights and bound around with ribbon to imitate doublet and hose. The lady of the house looked uncertain in purple velvet and a towering wimple. Her husband, the Sir Somebody, strode around beaming and talking to people, his spectacles contrasting oddly with his ruff and slashed knickerbockers. One had the feeling that every-body was sternly doing their duty. A large notice at the entrance had explained how ten thousand pounds must be raised for the repair of the village church.

'Actually,' said Martin, 'it's not all that bad, this. Not as good as stock-car racing, but there wasn't a hope of that . . .'

There were stalls (home-made sweets, at handsomely reduced prices), an archery competition in which you could have a go with a real cross-bow, a bran-tub with better-than-average loot, guessing the weight of an agitated sheep done up in pink ribbons (oh please, please may I win it, prayed Maria silently, please may I be the only person in our street with their very own Scottish Blackface sheep), coconut shies, and a Refreshment Tent where Mead was on sale only to those over eighteen. They had sandwiches and squash.

The afternoon grew hotter and noisier. There were a great many people, milling around the sweep of drive in front of the house, plunging off down the garden paths in search of Archery in the Kitchen Garden and Jousting First Left after the Stables. The friars had removed their dressing-gowns. Jerkins were peeled off to reveal Marks and Spencer shirts beneath. The lady of the house steamed gently beneath her purple velvet and the milkmaids serving in the Refreshment Tent grew pinker and more harassed. Maria, looking at the great, quiet, stone hulk of the house, longed suddenly for coolness. 'Let's go inside,' she said.

Conducted Tours of the Manor were one of the attractions offered. Martin looked doubtful, and then gave in. They went in through the front door in the wake of a dozen or so other people and the guide, a girl who seemed to live there.

Unencumbered by parents, a member of the Conducted Tour in her own right, Maria found herself looking at things with deep attention. At the Great Hall, from whose high stone walls protruded banners lacy with age; at stone steps dipping in the middle where feet had pattered down them always at the same place; at windows whose stone pillars sliced the Dorset landscape into three sections of greens and golds and blues; at worm-eaten chests and blocked-up arches and tattered silk chair covers.

And at pictures. Lagging at the back of the tour, she studied the dark oil-paintings in some huge room. Sir Henry Hope-Peverell— in tidy grey wig, his hand on a pile of books, a spaniel leaned lovingly against his leg: Lady Charlotte Hope-Peverell—with pearls and a lavish exposure of bosom; a girl in a blue dress, seated in a misty landscape, flowers scattered on her lap.

'You shouldn't have picked those,' said Maria reprovingly. 'They look like orchids to me.'

'Well, what would you do?' said the girl. 'Stuck here in a field all day having your picture painted.'

'Nobody's ever wanted to paint me,' said Maria. 'I like the way they've done your hair. All those curls.'

62

'It takes hours—people messing you about and telling you off when you complain. And just you try wearing this dress. Squashed in round the middle till I can hardly breathe. Ever tried climbing a tree in a skirt like this?'

'No,' said Maria. 'Did you live here?'

'Stuck here all my life,' said the girl gloomily.

'I should think you'd notice a few changes now. They've got a new electric stove in the kitchen. And a telly. I expect you'd have liked that.'

The rest of the party was moving out of the room. 'Come on,' said Martin.

''Bye,' said Maria to the girl.

'Goodbye,' said the girl. 'You're not missing anything, I can tell you. Horrible beastly portraits . . .'

Leaving the girl, frozen there forever in a gilt frame on a particular day of blue sky and cloud sometime long ago, Maria followed the guide around the rest of the house until finally they reached a door into the garden.

'Well,' said the guide cheerfully, 'that's about it. The bedrooms aren't very interesting.' One or two members of the tour looked disappointed.

Beyond the door was a small, walled garden. 'The herb garden was laid out in the time of Elizabeth I,' said the guide. 'I'm afraid it's a bit of a mess now. We never seem to get around to weeding it.' And, indeed, the outline of once-trim flower beds and paths was blurred with rampant greenery.

'There's supposed to be everything,' she added. 'All the English herbs. Marjoram and thyme and basil and all that sort of thing. Excuse me, I've got to do the next lot.'

They wandered through the garden, pinching leaves that smelt sharp, or sweet, or balmy, each different, a dictionary of smells. They could not put a name to them.

'Thyme,' said Martin, 'that's thyme. I know because it grows on

63

the cliffs.' He rubbed the leaves between his hands and buried his nose in them, gulping the smell. 'Nice . . .'

They can't be the same *plants* as in the time of Elizabeth I, thought Maria—whenever that was, which I'm not very sure about —not the same actual plants. Plants don't last that long. But their great-great-great-grandchildren, perhaps. Seeds of seeds of seeds. She brushed against the dead flower-head of some great bushy thing, and thistledown floated on to the path and grass. More seeds.

'Do you ever think about being other people?' she said to Martin, abruptly.

'Not specially. It's enough bother thinking about me. Let's have tea again.'

No, thought Maria sadly, I shan't tell him much about that girl who lived in our holiday house and collected fossils. Which is a pity, because interesting things are even more interesting when you share them with somebody else.

'All right,' she said, 'let's have tea again.'

In the tea-tent they were re-united with the rest of Martin's family (the younger ones all now lavishly stained with iced lolly, the older ones loudly clamouring for food, drink, money or all three).

'There's Jousting at four o'clock,' said Mrs Lucas. 'We'll see that and then we're off. You can go and get a good place, Martin—and mind James for me for a minute while I find the Ladies. Do you want to come, Maria?'

Maria decided that she did. The Ladies (an unappealing arrangement of buckets behind canvas curtains) was in what appeared to be the kitchen garden. Emerging between rows of cabbages Mrs Lucas said, 'There's this church we've been forking out for all afternoon. Let's have a look at it.'

They went through a gate in the garden wall and into the churchyard. Mrs Lucas shifted the baby from one hip to the other, trod a cigarette out on the path, and wandered into the church, followed by Maria.

64

It was much like any other church, as far as she could see, though Mrs Lucas seemed to find something to detain her about the stained glass windows, and a brass in the floor. Maria fidgeted, and hoped they were not missing the jousting.

Mrs Lucas stopped before a large marble memorial let into one of the walls. 'I say, what a horror!'

A lady, much draped in white marble, reclined upon a marble sofa. Across her lap stretched a boy of about ten, with a nightdress on, his eyes closed. He had a lock of marble hair across his forehead and a most angelic expression. The lady, though, on closer inspection, could be seen to be weeping white marble tears. On either side of her were clustered very fat cherubs, also weeping.

' "Erected by his Grieving Mother," ' read Mrs Lucas, ' "In Ever-Loving Memory . . ." What a ghastly piece of work.' She moved away to look at the font.

'I think it's beautiful,' said Maria, very quietly, too quietly for anyone to hear. Her eyes pricked with not unenjoyable tears—the kind of tears prompted by a sad book. She had sometimes thought herself of dying young. In moments of extreme resentment against her parents she had relished the thought of them weeping over a pathetic (but extremely grand) little tomb in some enormous cemetery, feeling sorry that they had been so cruel to her.

Mrs Lucas was going out of the church door now and Maria tore herself away from the white marble lady to follow her. Heading towards sounds of excitement from the field beyond the stables, they found themselves at the Jousting. Martin waved from a place at the front of the crowd. Maria went to stand beside him while Mrs Lucas departed in search of the rest of her family.

Jousting in 1975 did not bear a great deal of resemblance to the real thing. Silver-painted wooden poles took the place of lances, producing a series of dull thwacks as knight met knight, rather than a spirited clash of weapons. What armour there was looked distinctly theatrical and cardboard, though a valiant attempt had been made

65

to give a convincing air to banners and pennants, so that the whole spectacle was at least colourful, though the ponies and horses dragged into service had in one or two cases rather spoiled the effect by eating part of their trappings. But the event was not without drama, the result as much of the knights' efforts to cope with the molehills in the field as with their opponents. There were some satisfactory falls, at least one requiring medical attention, two broken lances, several loose horses and much exhortation and encouragement from the crowd before it was finally announced that the two winners-on-points would compete for the title.

'Do you suppose he wins the Lady Somebody?' said Maria. 'That's what it would have been in old-fashioned times.'

'Not nowadays,' said Martin. 'Bottle of whisky, more like. I don't expect he'd want her, really.'

The opposing knights lined up at the far ends of the field. The system was for the jousters to ride at each other, gathering speed as they went, much like (allowing for the detours made necessary by the molehills) two trains approaching each other along the same track, the object being to be the knight managing the first thwack with the lance which, with any luck, would unseat your opponent and make you the winner. Several encounters had ended inconclusively, with both contestants missing the target entirely, or being carried off at a tangent by uncooperative horses. This was disappointing to the spectators.

'I'm having the red one,' said Martin. 'His horse went in a straight line last time. Oh, James, stop *fussing* ...'

'I want my mum.'

'Go and find her then.'

'I feel sick.'

'Go to Mum, then.'

'I can't find her. You find her.'

'In a minute.'

James began to wail. Distantly, the knights began their charge, with a determined trot that picked up slowly to a canter. The crowd settled contentedly to watch.

'I want my mum . . .'

'Oh, shut up . . .' said Martin through clenched teeth. 'Look, James, look at the horses . . .'

They were twenty or thirty yards apart now, approaching in a satisfactorily straight line, lances nicely at the ready. It had all the makings of a most promising joust. Oh please, prayed Maria, may nobody get hurt specially not the horses but if somebody could fall off *without* getting hurt because that's exciting . . .

'There's my mum,' said James, pointing. And there, indeed, she was, on the opposite side of the field, separated from them by the width of the jousting course and the two lines of rope to keep the spectators off it.

'Sssh . . .,' said Martin. 'Cor—this is going to be good . . .' Both horses were at a steady gallop now.

'Mum!' said James, breaking away.

People of only four can move faster than you think, when they have a mind for it. He had ducked under the rope and was in the middle of the course, at roughly the point where the two horses would meet, before either Martin or Maria realized what he was going to do.

'Oh, no . . . that child . . .' said somebody beside them.

Martin was shouting, and then ducking under the ropes after James.

Maria closed her eyes, and there swam before the closed lids things as horrible as what she must surely see if she opened them. She stood there with shut eyes and heard commotion around her, and thudding hooves, and felt sick in her stomach and thought that this could not really be happening. It was a dream—no, a nightmare—and she would wake up.

She opened her eyes.

There were people, milling about in the middle of the field, and there was a man on a horse, some way away, yanking at the reins, and there was the other horse, wedged somehow against one of the posts from which the ropes were slung. And there was Martin. And there was his mother, running from the other side of the field.

And there was James, holding someone's hand, looking around in surprise at all the fuss.

It was not until later, as they were all once more in the car, on the way home, after the exclaiming and blaming and forgiving and the re-play of the final joust and the presentation to the victor (on points, since no one either scored a hit or fell off) of a ticket to the Cup Final, that what had happened—or rather, what hadn't happened hit Maria with full force.

It nearly wasn't like this at all. It nearly wasn't everybody going back after a nice day and thinking about what's for supper and I wonder what's on telly. It was almost absolutely awful. But because it wasn't you don't think about it any more. About what we might have been doing now instead of just going back, all squashed up in the car and everybody talking at once.

She looked at James, at his face (blotched pink with iced lolly), gazing serenely out of the window, and his plump tummy bulging over the waist of his jeans, and then at Martin, locked in ferocious argument with one of his sisters. It nearly wasn't like this at all. It nearly ended up as a quite different kind of day.

Later, muddled and sleepy, she could not tell her parents what she meant.

'But if he was all right—the little boy—then everything was fine. Presumably the horses dodged him, or someone pulled him out of the way.'

'It's just everything nearly being quite different,' said Maria.

'He shouldn't have been allowed to wander off, at that age,' Mrs Foster went on, with a hint of criticism.

'Why does one thing happen and not another?'

Mr and Mrs Foster were people who believed in questions being given a proper answer. Mr Foster in particular. His answers were long and detailed and by the end of them Maria had sometimes forgotten what the question was. She knew a great deal about what the Houses of Parliament are for and why it is necessary to go to school and the difference between Labour and Conservative people.

'Well . . .' said her father. He looked at Maria across the kitchen table, and then out of the window, and then back at Maria again. 'Religious people think . . .' he began, and then, 'It's a complicated sort of question . . .' and then, 'Not entirely easy to explain . . .' and finally, 'I don't know.' He picked up the newspaper and vanished behind it.

'Isn't it time you were off to bed?' said Mrs Foster.

Maria went upstairs to her room, in the tail-end of a day that might have been an entirely different one. Although, she thought, you could say that about every single day, which is unsettling. She got into bed, and during that shadowy period between being awake and falling asleep images floated through her head: a marble boy wept over by a marble lady, thistledown and fossils and a prancing black dog. And, most persistent of all, the presence of a girl her own age, called Harriet, who had gone to sleep in this house on other August nights, hearing the sea outside the window.

6

Harriet

'How long do trees live?' said Maria. 'Longer than people? Or not so long?'

'Depends,' said Martin.

That, she had discovered, was what he said when he did not know the answer to something. It was a little like the kind of thing her father said under the same circumstances. She looked speculatively at Martin, adding, in her imagination, two feet to his height, and clothing him in a dark office suit and white shirt like her father's.

'Why are you staring at me?'

'I was wondering,' said Maria, 'what you were going to grow up into.'

'A person, presumably.'

'But what kind of person . . .'

'Like I am now, but bigger.'

'No,' said Maria, 'I don't think it works like that.' She had once seen a photograph of her father when six years old, squatting with a shrimping-net over a rock-pool: that remote figure bore little relation to the person with whom she now lived. Quite apart from the fact that he was no longer interested in shrimping.

'It would be good to change into something else,' said Martin with interest. 'Like *Stomechinus* ending up as a sea-urchin. I'll be a race-horse. No, a jaguar.'

'It took *Stomechinus* millions and millions of years. And even then it didn't change all that much.'

'But we're cleverer. We should be able to find out how to speed it up.'

They were coming back from the beach, alone, after an unsuccessful fossil-hunt. They had rivals, they discovered. The beach echoed with discreet tappings as other addicts interfered with the blue lias. There were even apparent professionals with small sacks and geological hammers, collecting on an industrial scale: these they stalked resentfully, hating them.

'Actually,' Martin went on, 'it wouldn't work, of course, because jaguars only became jaguars because they had to run faster than anything else so as to catch things to eat.'

'P'raps people do that anyway?'

'What do you mean?'

'P'raps,' said Maria, 'they turn into the kind of people they are because the things that happen to them make them like that.' Which sounds a bit muddled, she thought, but *I* know what I mean. Like I'm shy and I talk to myself because of the sort of family I live with and Martin's like he is because he's got a different kind of family.

'I don't know what you're on about,' said Martin. 'You know something?' he added. 'You are a bit peculiar sometimes. You were talking to that tree yesterday. I heard. You were sitting in it and you suddenly said "Oh, *Quercus ilex* . . ." '

Maria went scarlet.

'I don't expect there's anything much you can do about it,' said Martin kindly. 'It doesn't bother me, anyway . . . Why did you want to know how long trees live?'

'I just wondered. I wondered how old my tree—our tree—is. The ilex tree.'

They reached their own road, stopping at the newsagent on the corner to buy sweets. They were now regulars here. It was that kind of convenient and all-providing shop that sells everything from fishing-rods and beach-hats to biscuits and brown envelopes. And,

71

Maria noticed for the first time, as the assistant shovelled pear-drops into the scales, postcards of the town of a kind that she had not seen before—not photographs but black and white pictures with people in old-fashioned clothes walking along the Cobb. In one, a group gazed shore-wards to a reduced version of today's town, in which the front looked much the same but the cliffs were not spread with houses. Sailing-boats like butterflies stood in a glassy sea. She tried to pick the point where their house should be, roughly, and found only fields.

'Fifteen pence,' said the assistant. 'Do you want the postcard, dear?'

Or, Maria now saw, you could have a whole collection of such cards made up into a calendar. Forty-five pence. Which, at the moment, she had not got, but, she remembered, might well have after tomorrow, when Uncle David was to come down, who invariably gave her fifty pence as a present.

'I think I'll save up for the calendar,' she said. August was topped by a picture of fishermen with nets, oddly dressed. September you could not see.

'Old prints,' said the assistant. 'Nineteenth century. People like that kind of thing, nowadays. They don't appeal to me so much, personally. Enjoying your holidays?'

'Super,' said Martin.

'Time flies. The fifteenth already. September before we know where we are.'

They came out into the street again, sucking pear-drops. It was lunch-time, and the population of the street's hotels, boarding-houses, and rented holiday houses converged upon them, laden with wet bathing-things, folding chairs and baskets. Amid these comings and goings, like a rock defying the fretful waters of a channel, stood the sombrely dressed figure of Mrs Shand, leaning slightly upon a stick, a shopping basket set upon the pavement beside her.

'That's our landlady,' said Maria apprehensively. Mrs Shand's gaze was beamed down the road towards her, but without any sign of recognition. This did not entirely surprise Maria; people usually did forget her quite quickly, she had found. To remain in people's heads you need to be noisy, or striking-looking, or memorable in some other way, and she was not. As they reached Mrs Shand she began to slide by between her and the garden hedge, at which point Mrs Shand's head swung sharply round in her direction.

'I know you, do I not?'

Maria explained.

Mrs Shand turned her attention to Martin. 'And who is this?'

Maria explained further.

'And what have you been doing with yourself, young man?' said Mrs Shand.

This daunting question, which, Maria knew, would have reduced her to silence, had no such effect upon Martin. He proceeded to tell Mrs Shand, at considerable length, so that she was obliged twice to shift her weight from one leg to the other, and prevented several times from interrupting him either to ask a question or bring his account to an end.

'If you are interested in fossils,' she said at last, 'you may, if you would like, come to see me and I will show you some very interesting specimens of my grandfather's.'

'O.K.,' said Martin.

'Yes, please,' said Mrs Shand reprovingly.

'That's quite all right,' said Martin. 'This afternoon, if I've got time. We've got to go now, it's lunch-time—'bye.' He treated Mrs Shand to an amiable grin. Maria, turning furtively as she went in at her drive gates, saw the old lady standing where they had left her. She looked in some indefinable way slightly less rock-like.

The Fosters spent what Mrs Foster called a 'quiet' afternoon in the garden (but our afternoons are never noisy, thought Maria, never

never, we just don't have that kind of afternoon . . .). Maria read, her father alternately read the newspaper and slept beneath it, and her mother sewed. She was making a patchwork quilt. She had been making it for eight years now: it was very large, exquisitely designed and sewn, and would surely be very beautiful when finished. Maria, when she was younger, had sometimes felt jealous of the patchwork quilt and once she had taken some of the pieces of material that her mother was collecting for it and put them in the bottom of the dustbin under tea-leaves and potato peelings. No one had ever known. It was quite the worst thing she had ever done and she still went hot and cold at the thought of it. Nowadays she no longer had any emotions of any kind about the quilt but it did sometimes occur to her that it was taking her mother almost as long to make it as it had taken to make her, Maria, and that people often showed more interest in the quilt.

From the other side of the hedge, from time to time, came the sounds of intermittent warfare between the Lucas children. There was some kind of long-term, all-afternoon quarrel going on which flared up periodically into shouted argument. Sometimes the argument would end in shrill and noisy weeping from one of the younger children. When this happened Mr Foster would frown and sigh, and Mrs Foster would look up from her sewing and stare with disapproval at the hedge separating the two gardens. Once she said, 'Those are really very uncontrolled children.' On two or three occasions the tears and arguments were brought to an abrupt and unnatural close by brief but loud interruption from one or other of the mothers. On these occasions Mr and Mrs Foster exchanged glances, and Mrs Foster turned back sternly to the quilt. Maria had never, she realized, heard either of them shout, at each other, her, nor anyone else. All this was quite interesting, and she lay alternately reading and thinking about it until it was time for tea.

Martin appeared as they were sitting round the table.

74

'Have you had tea, Martin?' said Mrs Foster.

Martin had, it appeared, but was quite open to suggestions about a second one. He sat down with them and ate four sandwiches and a slice of cake. He had a second slice when pressed—not very hard—by Mrs Foster.

'It's funny she's not fatter,' he said, nodding his head in Maria's direction. 'All this food just for her. Lucky thing.'

'More cake?' said Mrs Foster doubtfully.

'No, thank you,' said Martin, after a brief but apparently careful consideration. 'Shall we go and see that old lady?'

Maria was only moderately enthusiastic about this. Mrs Shand alarmed her, just a little. This time, though, she remembered, she would be fortified by Martin. One would not need to talk, just listen and look. And those clocks could do with looking at again.

'All right,' she said.

Outside the hotel, Martin expressed his deep contempt for that notice. 'Who do they think they are? No Children or Dogs . . . They'll be lucky.' He stumped loudly up the stairs.

Mrs Shand, when they arrived in her room, was engaged upon the same piece of pink embroidery. The effect of the room, its atmosphere, and the sight and sound of the clocks on Martin was, for a few moments at least, to silence him. He stood staring round, rubbing one plimsoll up and down against the grubby leg of his jeans.

Mrs Shand got up from the sofa and went over to a cabinet in one corner of the room, from which she took a shallow tray covered with a cloth.

'You may sit down and look at this. Please be careful where you put your feet, young man.'

Maria and Martin sat side by side upon a sofa blowsy with brown and yellow cotton roses, and examined the tray of fossils, while Mrs Shand observed, in silent irritation, the trickle of sand which marked Martin's progress across the room, and then returned to her sewing.

The fossils, they instantly recognized, were a cut above the ordinary. No *Gryphaea* or *Stomechinus* here, not even a solitary ammonite, but belemnites like huge bullets, sharks' teeth so large that the picture they conjured up of their Jurassic owners made Maria vow silently that she would never again set foot in the English Channel, and the most delectable crumpled lily-like plant etched upon a slab of rock.

'Cor . . .' said Martin lovingly.

'You may handle them,' said Mrs Shand (unnecessarily, for they already were).

'Who found this?' demanded Martin.

Mrs Shand lowered her spectacles and looked at him over the top of them. 'My grandfather. He was a friend of Sir Charles Darwin and helped him with his researches by collecting fossils on the cliffs here. I will show you a photograph of him.'

'Where did he find it?'

But Mrs Shand was back at the cabinet now, burrowing in a drawer quite silted up, Maria could see, with papers and bundles of letters. She returned carrying a large, apparently very old (for the leather was faded and here and there quite worn away) photograph album. She set this upon Maria's lap and turned the pages over until she came to one on which was a single photograph of an elderly man with a prolific white beard and kindly expression. The same person, Maria now saw, whose photograph stood upon the mantelpiece in the drawing-room of the house over the road. On the opposite page was another yellowed photograph of a lady in clothes both billowing and tightly buttoned, giving her the same densely upholstered effect as the Victorian chairs in the drawing-room of the holiday house. She wore a lace cap, and more frills of lace emerged at the neck and wrists of her dress. But her face, amid these oddities of dress, was an ordinary, comfortable, motherly face: you could see it today twenty times over in any High Street or supermarket. And a strand of hair had escaped from beneath her cap and lay across her forehead, adding a homely touch to the otherwise formal picture. People aren't different on the outside, Maria thought, people from other times. But the inside of their heads must be, because of everything being different all round them. She stared at the photograph, seeing also that the brooch at the person's neck, of clustered ivory roses, was the brooch worn now by Mrs Shand, seated in her chair on the opposite side of the fireplace, smoothing the embroidered panel upon her knee.

'My grandmother,' said Mrs Shand. 'If you turn the page you will see my mother as a small girl, and her younger sister Harriet.'

They sat upon one of those chairs from the drawing-room. Or rather, the older girl sat and Harriet stood beside it and leaned upon the arm. You could see that she had been told to stand thus, to make a nice picture. They were dressed alike in dresses of some dark material that came to below the knee, black boots which vanished into the dresses, buttoned with a multitude of tiny buttons, and white pinafores with an abundance of ruffle and frill. Their long hair, held back by bands, had just been brushed, by the look of it. They were alike—you could have known they were sisters—but the older girl was thinner and darker, and her expression the more solemn (or bored?). Harriet's face, on the other hand, which was fatter and, even in the brownish-yellow tones of the photograph, gave an impression of pink cheeks and blue eyes, had a clenched, stiff look about it which seemed somehow not at all natural. It came to Maria suddenly what this look suggested. She was going to start giggling, she thought. Something happened (the photographer, maybe—did he look funny, or make some funny remark?) and she giggled and they told her to stop it for the picture, or she was just going to giggle, and trying not to.

Maria stared intently at the picture, and Harriet, a hundred years and more away, suppressed unseemly laughter. In black ink, under the photograph, someone had written, 'H.J.P. and S.M.P., aged 10 years and 12 years, February 1865.'

'There are some more family groups,' said Mrs Shand, 'if you go on.'

There were indeed. Mother and children groups, with the baby (like a chrysalis swathed in white muslin) upon its mother's knee, and the other children ranged beside the chair in order of size; portraits of one person after another, head and shoulders emerging from a soft brown cloud; muzzy pictures of out-of-doors groups, playing croquet on some tree-fringed lawn, seated at tea round a table set beneath a tree, or, in one interesting case, sprawled on the beach amid a clutter of sunshades and tartan rugs. Behind them reared a most recognizable slice of cliff.

'That's here,' said Maria.

'Naturally,' said Mrs Shand, 'since they lived here. You may each have a chocolate, if you care for one.'

'Thanks,' said Martin with alacrity.

Individuals emerged now from the various photographs, as Maria turned the pages over. Here was the bearded father (holding a new baby, with an expression of kindly bewilderment upon his face), and here the plump mother again, festooned with small children. And here were Harriet and her sister. And here, a few pages on, was her sister, but taller, and alone this time. And here she was, again, with her hair piled upon her head and her skirt down to the ground, defined now by her dress as a grown-up person though her face looked much the same. She changed into something else, thought Maria, like butterflies. People don't do that now, you don't exactly know when they stop being children and are grown-up because everybody goes on wearing the same kind of things all the time. Martin's mother's jeans are just like mine. The old-fashioned arrangement seemed not at all a bad one. You'd know where you were, at least, she thought. And what you were.

She searched the pages for a grown-up, evolved Harriet, but could not find her. This was worrying. Here was Susan, looking fat and discontented, aged sixteen, and here she was again, wreathed in smiles, quite grown-up, with a baby in her arms. But no Harriet. Maria stared up at the sampler.

'She made the sampler, didn't she?' she said. 'Harriet.'

'Not entirely,' said Mrs Shand. 'Susan finished it. My mother.'

Maria opened her mouth to ask why but was interrupted by Martin, who had ignored the album and was still poring covetously over the fossils.

'Where did he find the fish?'

Dapedius colei, it was called, glinting in its slab of lias, a perfectly orthodox and scaly fish, like some Jurassic bream.

'I bet we'll never find one of them . . .' said Martin, in envious gloom.

'On the West Cliff, I believe,' said Mrs Shand, 'after a cliff-fall had exposed some fresh strata. That happens, you know, from time to time.'

Alluring as the fossils were, Maria found that her attention had somehow strayed entirely now to the album. She turned the pages back, learning from each group more of the family structure—the C.R.P. who must be an aunt, and the Miss D. who hung upon the fringes of a group, here and there (governess, nurse?), and the graded F.S.P.s and B.M.P.s and T.J.P.s who were all the other brothers and sisters. Susan and Harriet seemed to come around the middle of the family. She went back to that early picture and studied them both again: it was the only good one of Harriet. Elsewhere she was an indistinct member of a group and after the middle of the album did not seem to appear at all.

'Would you like a chocolate, Mrs Shand?' said Martin with an air of sudden concern.

'Not just now, thank you.' Martin's hand hovered above the silver box, and there was a pause while Mrs Shand looked at him over her spectacles, saying nothing but apparently savouring the moment.

Then she said, 'Very well, young man. One more,' and Martin's hand foraged among the chocolates and Mrs Shand returned to her sewing.

Maria got up and went over to the sampler. She thought that it must have been very difficult to sew. The stitches were small and neat, with never a mistake, as far as you could see—it must have taken hours and hours. Hours and hours, perhaps, when the person sewing it would have much preferred to be doing something else. Because I wouldn't like to have to do that, thought Maria, not one little bit. Though I'd have put the tree in, too, and its name underneath—*Quercus ilex*—and the fossils. And the little black dog. And the swing (the swing? what swing?), and the urns. And the house. Because of course it is the house, only for some reason she made it brown and not white, but otherwise it's much the same. Which, Maria thought, I find odd—it being there then and still here now but Harriet isn't. And, thinking of Harriet with sudden intensity, she looked back to the sampler again.

She was looking sideways at it, and the sampler itself had become suddenly invisible, for the glass behind which it was framed reflected the window at the other side of the room, and the view out of the window, so that from this angle she saw only a reflected square of garden with lawn and trees swaying softly in the wind. And, suddenly, like a portrait in a frame—a photograph even, but coloured this time, and quite real, she felt sure—a face, a pink and white face with fair hair held back by a band, above a frilled white pinafore, staring at her out of the sampler.

But no, in at the window. Because it is back to front, she thought, a reflection . . . And she turned sharply round, to find herself looking at a window empty of anything save lawn, trees and sky . . .

She swung round to look at the sampler again—and it had become nothing now but canvas and stitching once more. And a reflection, if you found the right angle, but a reflection of nothing more surprising than window, trees . . .

80

'What a very fidgety person,' said Mrs Shand. 'Round and round . . . You are making me dizzy.'

Maria sat down guiltily.

'Perhaps you would kindly put the album back in the cabinet. And the fossils, if you have seen enough of them.'

'Thank you for having us,' said Martin, when this was done.

Mrs Shand waved her needle with a gesture of gracious dismissal. 'Please see that the door closes properly behind you.'

'Excuse me,' said Maria, 'please, why did Susan . . .'

But the rest of the question was lost. Mrs Shand, looking up as she spoke, interrupted before she had finished.

'And perhaps you would kindly mention to your mother that the side gate into the garden is inclined to squeak. If the noise offends it should be oiled. Did you say something?'

'No,' said Maria.

'Super fossils,' said Martin, as they crossed the road back to their own side.

'Mmn.'

'That fish thing. *Dapedius* . . .'

'Yes.'

'I'm going to find one of those,' said Martin.

'Oh,' said Maria, without conviction.

'Don't you believe me?'

'Oh, yes,' said Maria hastily.

Martin went back to the hotel to watch television. Maria walked round the side of the house, across the lawn (the lawn upon which, possibly, in fact probably, a large noisy family had played croquet, and then lined up against the wall to have their photograph taken, smallest in front, mother and father and aunts and others in the middle). She climbed up to her favourite branch in the ilex, and for the next half hour she sat in the tree and told it things (but silently, in her head). A very peculiar thing happened just now, she said to

81

it, I thought I saw Harriet's face looking out of the sampler she made, as though she was still here.

And don't, she said to the tree with sudden passion, don't tell me it was all my imagination. Because I don't believe it. Like I don't believe in her being grown-up, like Martin said she was. I think . . . I think something happened to her, but I don't know what.

The thought trailed away into a whisper, among the whispering leaves of the tree.

7

An Afternoon Walk and a Calendar

Once, when Maria was younger, she had imagined a burglar. She had imagined him on to the ledge outside her window, and clothed him in dark furtive clothes, and given him a stocking over his head that horribly blunted his features as in a picture she had once seen in a newspaper. And then somehow he had got out of control, this burglar, and instead of staying where he was or dissolving like a nightmare as you wake, he had tampered with the catch of the window so that lying in bed she distinctly heard it click, and the window lift, and then there he was climbing into the darkness of the room, and she had huddled there first quaking and then finally screaming at full pitch till people came, lights snapped on . . . And then, of course, the burglar picked his moment to vanish, leaving Maria hysterical in an empty room.

But I have grown out of that kind of thing now, she thought. I can deal with burglars, and the stairs creaking in the night, and thunderstorms. I can even go to the bathroom in the dark if I can't find the electric light switch. I am on the way to being grown-up and not having problems of that kind at all.

'That's what you think,' said the cat. 'What about the time you lost your head in the supermarket and rushed about weeping?'

'That was different,' said Maria. 'I couldn't find my mother. I thought she'd gone without me.'

'A pretty poor performance, all the same,' said the cat. 'Grown-up my foot . . .'

It was sitting at the foot of the ilex tree, grooming its belly in a contorted attitude that involved sticking one leg vertically above its head.

'You've missed a bit,' said Maria, 'on your left side.'

The cat began a vigorous lathering of its ears. 'I take it you won't be mentioning to that boy that you see faces in old samplers?'

'He's not all that interested in her, actually,' said Maria.

'Got some sense. Unlike you.'

'I don't see why it's not sensible to be interested in other people,' said Maria coldly.

'Well, what could be more silly than spending your time chuntering on about a girl you've never known and never will. You could be reading a good book. Improving your mind. Learning something.'

'Speak for yourself,' snapped Maria.

'Ah,' said the cat, 'but I can't. Remember?' It flexed its claws, apparently admiring them. 'What's so fascinating about her, anyway? A perfectly ordinary child, no doubt, like yourself.'

'I don't think she ever grew up.'

'Rubbish. Everyone does.'

'They don't have to,' said Maria stiffly. After a moment she went on, 'There are no photographs of her any older than I am now. And her sister finished the sampler.'

'Plenty of explanations for that.'

'And funny things happen here, so that you can't be quite sure what's real and what isn't. There's a dog that barks but nobody seems to have a dog around here. And I hear this swing that squeaks.'

'The gate needs oiling,' said the cat. 'Old Mrs Thing said. 'Remember?' It prowled away into the undergrowth, ears flattened, and Maria said to its back view, angrily, you don't care, do you? You don't care what happened to her. Nobody does, except me. Because I think something happened, and that's why she didn't grow up. And with this thought nagging at the back of her mind

84

like a painful tooth she slid down the last three feet of the tree and landed with a thump on the grass.

Uncle David and Aunt Ruth had arrived. In consequence, there was more lunch than usual and it was eaten in the dining-room. Maria was kissed, and obligingly kissed people back. She was told that she had grown, and could find nothing to say in response: her uncle and aunt had not visibly changed in any way, so that there was no comment she could make of that kind, unless she was to point out that Aunt Ruth's hair was untidy, or that Uncle David had cut himself shaving, which would have seemed rude. Only grown-ups, she had learned, are allowed to make remarks about what people look like: if children do so it is rude.

That being done, she found herself forgotten. She was talked over and around, which she did not mind since it allowed her to get on with various things she wanted to think about. At the end of lunch Uncle David remembered her suddenly and said, 'Time Maria and I had a private word,' which he had said on every visit as far back as she could remember and which meant he was about to give her fifty pence. He rummaged in his pocket and for a nasty moment she thought he was going to go on to say, 'Dear me, now what can that be behind your right ear?', which meant that he was going to conjure the fifty pence out of her hair, as he always used to do when she was younger. She stood there resignedly, waiting for this, and the resigned expression must have turned into her cold one, for Uncle David hastily handed over the fifty pence and began to talk to her father.

After lunch they went for a walk. They started out over the fields to the west of the house, following the path that led to the cliff walk from Lyme to Axmouth. Aunt Ruth made exclaiming noises about how lovely it all was. Uncle David lit his pipe and left behind him an aromatic wake of pipe smoke. Maria's father instructed the visitors upon the history and topography of the town. Her mother

85

told Aunt Ruth about some material she was thinking of recovering the best chairs in when they went home.

Maria fell behind. Presently she was some twenty paces from the others, which allowed her to get on with her own thoughts without having to be interrupted by what other people were saying. She felt quite alone in this sunlit airy place, suspended between the mysterious depths of the sky above and the restless shimmering of the sea. Stopping for a moment, and looking back, she could see the rooftops of the town spilling down to the shore between green flanks of hill, and, beyond it, a landscape neatly squared off into fields, with the town fingering out into it, spawning houses along the roads. And underneath it all, thought Maria, there's rock, our blue lias, full of ammonites and belemnites and everything. People dump houses on it, and petrol stations, and churches, and branches of Tesco, and underneath it all the place stays what it was in the beginning, before everything, millions and millions of years ago . . .

About a hundred and forty million years, for instance, like those pictures in the museum said. On a Saturday afternoon then (if they bothered with Saturdays, that is) there'd have been pterodactyls flying around instead of seagulls, and ichthyosauruses on the beach instead of people's dogs. And ammonites everywhere, like we have flies now—no, like herrings because they were in the water, of course.

'Maria . . .'

'Coming,' said Maria, without having heard, dawdling along the path, which had left the fields now and wound among trees. How very peculiar, she thought. There are places, and they go on for ever and ever. And there are people (and dinosaurs and things) and they don't. And there are days and months and years (and centuries, in millions). The fossils are here, and Harriet, and me, like beads on a necklace. One after another, and yet all at once.

'Maria, *will* you hurry up!'

86

They were standing waiting for her at a point where the path plunged off into deeper woodland.

'Tired, dear?' said Aunt Ruth kindly, and Maria stared at her with a blank cold face, not because she felt either blank or cold but because a torrent of thought was still going through her head about places, pterodactyls and a girl who made a sampler.

'*Maria . . .*' said her mother, and Maria jumped and said no thank you she wasn't tired at all.

'Onward?' said Mr Foster, and there was a break for discussion while everyone said what they thought about going onward or not. Mr Foster and Uncle David were in favour of it. Mrs Foster wanted to be back not too late to get the supper on. Aunt Ruth thought the path looked a bit steep and wondered about her shoes. A notice said that you could walk to Axmouth and back, but it would take you three or four hours and be very strenuous, which was perhaps why Aunt Ruth gazed longingly back towards Lyme Regis.

'Just part of the way,' said Mr Foster, 'until we start to flag. The weak may fall by the wayside.' He set off briskly between the trees.

Maria dropped behind once more and returned to this question of places. Can places, she wondered, like clocks, stop? So that a moment goes on, as it were, for ever—like the ammonites suspended in a piece of rock. I wish it *was* like that, she thought, how interesting that would be. As interesting as if you could see into other people's heads, seeing backwards like that, as it were, into somebody else's time. And she seemed to see again that reflected face in the glass of the sampler.

'Careful, here,' called Mr Foster, 'rather a steep bit . . .' and there was a little flurry of activity ahead as Aunt Ruth, in unsuitable shoes, slithered on the shaly surface of the path, nearly fell, and was set to rights again by Uncle David.

It was another of those days when bands of sunlight fled along the coast and huge heaps of cloud roamed the sky. In the language of weather forecasting, of course, it would be a day of sunny periods, with perhaps the suggestion of a scattered shower. In any other language, it was a day of gold and palest blue and chestnut brown in which shadows chased across a chameleon sea that melted from turquoise to sombre grey and back to milky green. But the sea was hidden for the most part by the thick belt of trees and bushes through which they walked along a path that climbed and then suddenly dropped again. At each side of the path wild plants arranged themselves according to preference, tall things in clumps that swayed before the wind, creeping things that swarmed over low rocks and nestled down in the grass. Grass vetchling, thought Maria, I know that one now, and this green thing like a little pine tree is giant horsetail—we looked that up in the flower book—and that's spurge and that's lesser celandine. And, examining this tangle of growth, she was struck by the orderliness of it all, the way in which each plant knows its place and sticks to it. A pocket of rich damp earth for one; a sandy shelf for another. Which, for things that can't think, seemed really rather clever. A shower of thistledown drifted away down to the sea. Waste, thought Maria sternly, not so clever.

These ups and downs, she realized, these great bites out of the ground that were giving Aunt Ruth so much trouble (as the path got rougher and steeper her murmurings about how late she thought it might be getting grew louder and stronger) must be old landslides. But very old, years and years ago, because all was covered now in trees and bushes. And now they went steeply down and came to a place where the trees were yet taller and older, their reptilean roots lying exposed across the path (and proving yet another hazard to poor Aunt Ruth). And the things that grew were different also. Ferns and wild garlic and a strange primeval reed-like plant with drooping head.

'Oh dear,' said Aunt Ruth breathlessly. 'Up we go again . . .'

It was very quiet. From time to time a pigeon lurched from one tree to another. Leaves rustled. A seagull sailed over somewhere out of sight, with a sad trailing cry. Otherwise there was nothing to be

88

heard but the sound of their own footsteps and Uncle David talking to Maria's father.

And then, suddenly, a dog barking. No, thought Maria, yapping not barking. A bark is the loud important noise that big dogs make. This is the noise that a small dog makes, a rather silly small dog, the kind that runs round and round in circles and gets over-excited. And she looked round for the dog, which was quite clearly here, and yet nowhere to be seen, in this tipping, shelving place of trees and bushes. And as she realized this it came to her, slowly but somehow not all that surprisingly, that this was the dog she had heard barking from the garden back at the holiday house.

She caught up with the others.

'There's a dog got lost somewhere. Yapping and yapping.'

They stopped, and without footsteps the place was quite still, with only wind and sea and bird noises. And this dog.

'Where, dear?'

'Here,' said Maria, in an off-hand voice, 'somewhere just near.' Poor little dog, it was really in a dreadful state, quite hysterical.

They looked all round, and at each other, the four of them. Uncle David shook his head in a bewildered manner and set about re-lighting his pipe, a tricky process of putting himself between the wind and the lighted match.

'Well,' said Mrs Foster, 'I'm afraid I can't hear anything.'

Maria looked at them blankly, listening to the dog.

'Of course,' said Aunt Ruth, 'she may have much keener hearing. You'd expect it, at that age.'

The dog was working itself up into a most dreadful frenzy. It's not lost, thought Maria, that's not what's the matter. It's that something's happening that's upsetting it. And even as she thought this the noise of the dog was swamped by another noise, a kind of rushing and tearing and slipping noise as though all of a sudden the whole world was on the move, and through it, just, came the anguish of that distraught dog, and someone shouting. Children shouting.

'Oh . . .' said Maria, with this noise in her ears, and as it gathered and drowned everything she found herself clutching the thin trunk of a tree beside the path, for suddenly the very ground under her feet seemed no longer quite reliable.

'Maria, whatever is the matter?' said her father crossly, and as he said it the noise stopped, and the dog too, and the path became quite steady again and Maria let go of the tree.

'Nothing,' she said.

And she bent down to do up the strap of her sandal which was tiresomely flapping. For there was nothing any more. And with the world quite solid again, and the dog vanished and that other strange noise with it, the whole business seemed not quite real, just as yesterday the face of that girl in the glass of the sampler seemed an instant later as though it had perhaps not been there at all.

'Well,' said Uncle David, 'push on, shall we?'

But Aunt Ruth had had enough. She didn't want to be a drag and of course everyone else must carry on, she'd be quite happy to sit here for a bit (with an unenthusiastic glance at the undergrowth of bramble and nettles) but she did feel perhaps time was pressing rather.

And so they all turned round and set off back again, with Aunt Ruth at the back, becoming noticeably silent on the uphill bits, and Maria in front this time, because the feelings she had just been having for some reason made her want to get back too.

At the corner of their road she remembered the fifty pence in her pocket, and the calendar that she had already promised herself, and she went into the shop and bought it. Her father and Uncle David broke off their conversation as she came out to look down at her with kindly interest.

'Well,' said her father, 'and what's Maria been squandering her pennies on?'

'A nice drawing-book, I expect,' said Aunt Ruth.

They gazed at the calendar in surprise. 'Very nice,' said Uncle

David. 'Good old-fashioned pictures, eh? Reminds you of Dickens and that sort of thing. Very pretty.'

'That's what you really wanted?' said Mrs Foster.

What she means, of course, thought Maria, is that she can't imagine why. And turning over the pages of the calendar, from one greyish picture to another, she could quite see how it would appear to someone else, humbly competing with those handsome coloured views of selected bits of Dorset, immaculately photographed cottages and cliffs and downland scenes.

'Turns the clock back a bit, eh?' said Uncle David, looking over her shoulder, and Maria gave him a startled glance.

September, she now saw, offered a view of the town and the coastline to the left, as though someone had sat a half-mile or so offshore in a fishing-boat to draw it. The cliffs were covered with trees, thickly, as now.

'Let's see . . .' said Uncle David. 'We'd be about there, yes?' and his large finger came down at a point on the picture at the edge of Lyme. 'Town's spread a bit since then. Only two or three houses along there in those days.'

'One of them's ours,' said Maria.

'Is that so?' said Uncle David doubtfully. He peered more closely at the picture. 'Not really clear enough to be sure about that.'

'It is,' said Maria.

'And that's where we've just been walking. Been a bit of cliff erosion since, by the look of it.'

And about that he was perfectly right, for the picture showed a more regular coastline than the steeply shelving woods in which they had just been walking. So at least some of that happened since the picture was made, thought Maria, I wonder when? And looking at the bottom corner of the print she saw 1840 in small sloping letters.

Since 1840, anyway, and Susan and Harriet weren't even born then, because Susan finished the sampler in 1865. In September 1865. But those trees we walked through were quite old so it didn't happen all that long after. I wonder, she thought, I wonder if . . . And a thought, a disturbing thought, came into her head and hung there like a grey cloud until Uncle David spoke again.

'Interesting,' said Uncle David, 'seeing how a place changes, that kind of thing . . .'

'Yes,' said Maria warmly, and for an instant there passed between them a sympathy that quite blotted out the fact that Maria was eleven and Uncle David really quite old, and that usually they could not think of anything much to say to each other.

'Maps, now,' said Uncle David vaguely, 'get a lot out of old maps, myself. Not your aunt's cup of tea so much, of course. Must show you a book I've got sometime.'

Maria nodded, meaning that she would like that very much. Aunt Ruth, who had been saying to Mrs Foster, as Maria had clearly heard on the edges of her own conversation with Uncle David, 'Such funny taste for a little girl—old prints . . .' turned round suddenly and said, 'Well, on our way, I think, dear . . .' Which meant that she wanted to bustle them both back off home to London. Aunt Ruth, Maria had noticed before, was a person who felt unsafe if detached too long from London. She plunged beyond it, briefly, rather as a nervous swimmer plunges into the sea with head turned always towards the shore.

And after that there was a flurry of farewells, and more kissing and being kissed. And then the visitors were gone and the Foster family subsided once more into a private calm. Maria hung the calendar up in her room, with the other months folded behind the August page, and as she did so it occurred to her that it was, in a sense, something of a bad bargain since most of the year was already gone. There is nothing so lifeless as an old calendar, unless it be last year's diary. Which, Maria thought, is a bit silly, because time isn't uninteresting just because it's time that has been had, rather than time that is still to come. And she looked back through the other pages of the calendar, and thought as she did so of her own January (when she had had chickenpox) and March (her birthday, and the month in which she started to have skating lessons) and June (containing her first train journey alone, to visit her godmother). Those months seemed like the filled and labelled jam-jars in the larder at home: the rest, September and October and their neighbours, stood empty and unpredictable.

8

The Swing

'What we really need,' said Martin, 'is some old curtains. Or a rug or something.' He looked speculatively across the grass at the kitchen window to where Mrs Foster's head could be seen above the sink, attending to the washing-up.

'I don't think it would be much good,' said Maria, 'asking.'

'Is she in a bad mood?' Martin was an expert on the moods of his mother. He observed her with the professional interest of a weather forecaster, and laid his personal plans according to what the outlook seemed to be.

'Not specially,' said Maria. 'It's just she wouldn't let us have things out of somebody else's house.'

They were making a camp in the shrubbery, to the intense indignation of the cat, whose private jungle this was, for the molesting of the bird and mouse life therein. It sat on the edge of the lawn, staring resentfully at them and twitching the tip of its tail. Maria, trotting to and fro as she carried out Martin's instructions, avoided it as far as possible.

'Oh, well,' said Martin, 'never mind. We'll have to make a roof out of sticks and things. You get in that thick bit there and see what you can find.'

Maria, wriggling on her stomach through an especially resistant bush, thought how peculiar it is that one does not mind being ordered about by certain people. Indeed, one can positively enjoy it. Even when, as in this case, it involved being beaten around the head by the branches of a bush which seemed actually to have a life of its own. Oh, bother, she thought, as a leafy switch came lashing back into her face, and then, out loud 'Ow . . .' as her knee caught on something hard and sharp which rent a triangular tear in her jeans.

'What's the matter?'

'I cut my knee,' said Maria, fighting back tears and sitting down where she was in this inhospitable bush. The rip in her jeans would have to be sorted out later on with her mother. Beneath it was a pink graze on her knee, which, as she examined it, began to ooze blood. She looked down at the ground to see what it was she had come up against.

It was a piece of rusty iron, with a smattering of black paint clinging to it here and there, which reached away beyond her farther into the shrubbery. Attached to it was a length of thick chain. She gave this a pull and it came lifting up from the leafmould with, attached to it, an oblong of black metal in which was punched a pattern of holes.

Martin's face appeared through the leaves. 'Are you all right?'

'Yes.'

'You can mop it up on my shirt.'

'Thank you,' said Maria humbly.

'What's this thing?'

'I don't know.'

'Let's get it out. It might be useful.'

With something of a struggle, they got the lengths of metal, the chain, and the attached oblong out on to the grass. It was heavy and there was a good deal of it. Once there, it looked like the collapsed framework for some unidentifiable piece of industrial machinery. Martin heaved it around thoughtfully, and finally sat down and looked at it. He was, Maria knew, considering its future rather than its past, and, thinking of this, everything suddenly fell into place with beautiful clarity.

'It's a swing,' she said.

Martin stared.

'Those are the side bits, and the chains hang from that bar, and that thing with holes in it is the seat. Was the seat.'

'Actually,' said Martin, after a moment, 'you're right.'

'I know,' said Maria.

Like I've always known it was here somewhere, she thought. Because it's been making noises to tell me it was (and all right I know it's impossible for it to do that buried away under a whole lot of leaves lying on its side but it did, and that's that). And of course, she thought, it's their swing—Susan's and Harriet's. Their swing that they put in the sampler. The dog and the swing, I've been hearing them both . . .

'Come on,' said Martin, 'let's get going . . .'

All thoughts of the camp were abandoned. They laid the framework of the swing out on the lawn in its correct position and then, with much heaving and three pinched fingers between them got it up on its feet. It lurched at an uncomfortable angle owing to the fact that one of the bars separating the supports on one side had lost a screw and hung down uselessly, and the seat was not properly attached to the chain in one place. And it was rusty. Otherwise it was magnificent.

'Screwdriver,' said Martin. 'And screws. And black paint. And two brushes. And stuff for scraping rust off. Go and ask her.'

'Only if I have first go,' said Maria decidedly.

Martin stared for a moment as though he thought he could not have heard her right. Then he said, 'O.K. But hurry.'

'You won't get on it while I've gone? Promise?'

'What on earth's the matter with you?'

'I found it,' said Maria. 'It's mine. But you can share it,' she added.

'Thanks,' said Martin, in not quite his usual voice.

At least, she thought, as she rushed into the house, it's theirs really but it's mine as though I'd kind of inherited it, and I know they wouldn't mind that in fact I should think they'd be quite pleased if we get it all nice again.

'You want *what*?' said Mrs Foster, looking out of the window in surprise at what had suddenly blossomed upon the lawn in the middle of this August Thursday afternoon. 'Good heavens, Maria, what have you got hold of . . .?'

Screws and screwdriver could be managed, it seemed. Black paint and brushes were another matter. Mrs Foster, out in the garden, watched with apprehension while Martin ministered to the swing with tools and an expression of ferocious concentration.

'If you could just wait till this evening, Martin, when Maria's father gets back, he'd do it all for you and I would feel happier really if . . .'

'*No* . . .' said Maria in anguish and her mother, quelled by the passion in her voice, stood back and watched in a nervous silence.

'There,' said Martin. 'It's safe now . . .' He put a hand on the seat and pressed. The swing, foursquare on its feet now, stood firm in the middle of the lawn and sent a long, elegant shadow, pierced and patterned where the ironwork of the swing was pierced and patterned, streaming down the lawn in the late afternoon sunshine. 'Go on. Try it.'

'No,' said Maria. 'Not till it's finished. Painted and all.'

'*Painted* . . .' said Mrs Foster doubtfully. 'Really I'm not at all sure that I . . .'

'The shop on the corner,' said Martin to Maria.

'I've got sixty-five pence holiday money still . . .'

'Mum owes me last week's pocket-money. And forty pence she borrowed yesterday.'

They had gone before Mrs Foster could marshal her misgivings. In the shop, choice and decision confronted them. There is not just

97

paint, it seemed. There is paint that is non-drip and paint that is vinyl or emulsion and paint that is specially good for this, that or the other.

'*Shiny* paint,' said Maria. 'The shiniest kind of black paint.'

'We don't mind a bit of drip,' said Martin. 'Actually we quite like it.'

'Gloss,' said the assistant. 'You want a high gloss black enamel. Pint or half-pint?'

'Pint,' said Martin. 'And sandpaper. Two bits.'

The problem of the brushes nearly wrecked the whole thing. There was only enough money for one very small one. But then, after a feverish hunt, another was found in a box of junk at the back of a cupboard in the house, and they were equipped.

'You rub it down first,' said Martin. 'I know. I've seen my dad. Otherwise the paint doesn't go on properly.'

They rubbed, as the shadow of the swing grew longer and then was engulfed in a huge tide of shadow that came creeping down the lawn from the house. And then when they had rubbed they began to paint and as the sun sank slowly behind the house they painted away there in a companionable silence interrupted by nothing but the swish of their brushes and the distant, satisfactorily distant, noise of the rest of Martin's family squabbling in the next door garden.

'Great . . .' said Martin once, with a long, succulent sweep of the brush down a leg of the swing, and Maria nodded. Because painting, she had already decided, was in fact one of the very best things she had ever done. Out of all the many things that she had never done before. Better, almost, than swimming in a swimming-pool. Or skating.

'I'm doing the seat,' she said. 'Please.'

'O.K.' said Martin.

There is the moment you dip the brush in the paint, and tap it on the edge to get rid of the drips, and there it is all lush and fat with

paint in your hand, ready for the stroke down that sad, hungry, unpainted surface. And there is the moment you lay it on the dull,
unpainted surface, and what was rusty and tattered is transformed
with one majestic sweep into glistening sparkling black. And there
is the dabbing at the links of the chain to make them all neat and
painty once more, and the picking out of every curl and flourish of
the swing's seat, and the lying on your back to get at the underneath . . .

'That's it,' said Martin.

They stood back and surveyed it. It gleamed. It shone. It was re-
born. It had died and been buried under a bush and now it was
re-born. It was brand new. Brand, shining, black new. It was made
yesterday.

'It must be quite old,' said Martin.

'It's more than a hundred years old,' said Maria. 'Quite a bit more.
You see they . . .' and she stopped. 'I just know,' she said.

'Tomorrow,' said Martin, 'when it's dry . . .' and she nodded.
'Early. Straight after breakfast.' And he was gone, through the
hedge and back to the hotel to explain to his mother about the black
paint that had, most perversely, appeared all over arms, legs, faces,
shoes, jeans . . .

And even, as Maria discovered, standing at her window in the
twilight, in one's hair. She tugged at the comb until her eyes smarted,
and then, guiltily, abandoned the problem and her uncombed hair
with it. Maybe it would melt out, somehow, during the night. She
looked out at the swing, slowly disappearing now into the dusk
that crept over the garden so that what had been lawn merging into
the gloom of the shrubbery and encircling trees was now all one
single pool of darkness with the swing just holding its own as a
darker outline in the centre. And then the light ebbed away still
more so that she could not really see the swing, and she put her light
out and got into bed. She slept profoundly, except that once
she woke in the night to hear a wind stirring the trees and gently

rattling the window, and, above that, the melancholy noise of the swing.

And this time, she thought, falling away into sleep again, I'm not imagining it, whatever I may have been doing before. Because it's out there, real, and tomorrow I'm going to have first go on it.

She was tempted, in the morning, to rush straight out and on to it. She did, indeed, go out before breakfast, and the sun was shining and that wind in the night had made the paint as hard and dry as bone, with a glorious satin feel to it as you slid your hand down the shafts, or over the seat. But she resisted the temptation, ate her breakfast, and then sat at the edge of the lawn waiting for Martin.

He came at last.

'It needs oiling. I could hear it squeaking in the night.'

'It always squeaked,' said Maria.

'I don't know what you mean.'

'It doesn't matter. All right, we'll oil it.'

There was a pause. 'Go on,' said Martin.

She sat on the seat. It was hard, and she could feel through her jeans the patterning of the iron, holes and curls and lines (how odd that you can *feel* a pattern even if you can't see it . . .), and the warmth of it, from the sun.

'Shall I push you?'

'No,' said Maria.

She began to work at it, leaning back and putting her legs out straight in front and pulling at the chains, and it swung, in wider and wider sweeps. She was leaving the lawn, and Martin standing down there watching her, and flying up and up, so that at the peak of each sweep she hung for an instant looking down at the house and the ilex tree and the brick terrace behind the house with its plants in pots—no, urns, those things are called—that somehow you didn't normally notice from down below, on the same level. Like, somehow, the ilex tree looked very much smaller from up here, quite a young tree, really, without that great thick trunk and branches like armchairs . . . And the house looked different too, more like the house in the sampler, brown not white. She worked harder, pulling and letting go at just the right moment so that the swing flew up and bucked for a moment at the end of its flight, and then swept back again so that her skirts which had belled out as she went up, letting a gale of glorious cool air up her legs, went swishing down again, and the hair which had streamed away backwards came forward all over her face . . . Up and down, backwards and forwards, carving half-circles to and fro above the grass, an upward climb, and then a lovely shivery descent, rushing feet first down to the ground again, and then forward and up only to be snatched back and down again in a breathtaking swoop, skirt and pinny flying, hair everywhere now because her band had come off and blown away down the lawn. I want to go on doing this for ever and ever, she thought, I'll never stop, I'll stay here for ever swinging, I'll always be here . . .

And thinking this she paid no attention to someone who stood shouting, 'It's my turn now. It's not fair, Harry, it's my turn.' She pretended not to hear, swooping down and up, down and up, her feet skimming the grass before she flew up again level with the trees and the sky itself, it seemed, away from Susan down there wanting her turn and Fido rushing round in circles yapping . . .

'It's my turn!'

'What?'

'I said,' said Martin, 'It's my turn. You've had *ages* . . .'

She stopped leaning back, and let her legs sag, and the flights of the swing sagged also down and down until it was just rocking a little, and she was sitting there staring at Martin and the great brooding presence of the ilex tree and the crisp white back of the house and the brick terrace (crumbling rather, with clumps of grass pushing up through the brick—no urns) and Martin, scowling somewhat.

'What on earth's the matter? You look most peculiar.'

'So do you,' snapped Maria, tears suddenly springing to her eyes. And she slid off the swing, caught and ripped her jeans again on a jutting piece of iron as she did so, and went running into the house and up to her room.

From where, two remorseful hours later, she came back down into the garden in search of him. Recovering from a surge of emotion is like recovering from a sudden attack of fever. You are left feeling exhausted, ill-used, and, in Maria's case, distinctly guilty as though the illness were entirely your own fault as a result of eating too much rich and forbidden food. Because she was not, as it happened, a bad-tempered person, in the normal way of things. And, in all fairness, it had been Martin's turn. Accordingly, it was in a shrivelled and tormented state that she lurked by the gap in the hedge, waiting till he should appear in the hotel garden. The cat, with something unpleasant that it had taken from the dustbin, squatted under a bush and made remarks about people who were nasty to their friends.

He arrived just before lunch, with wet hair, straight from the beach.

'I'm sorry,' said Maria.

'What about?'

And as he said it, honestly wanting to know, it occurred to her that for someone as used as Martin to the kaleidoscopic emotions of a large family, an outburst of temper a couple of hours ago is really neither here nor there. It is digested, along with the last meal.

'I'm sorry I was cross and didn't let you have your go on the swing.'

'That's all right,' said Martin cheerfully. 'I did, anyway. Good, isn't it?'

'Super,' said Maria.

And they swung, alternately, five minutes each, until it was time for lunch.

The afternoon was spent on the beach with the Lucases. Mrs Foster was always pleased (if faintly guilty) to accept an offer for Maria to go off with them, thus excusing her the beach and freeing her for a contented and solitary afternoon with the patchwork quilt.

'It's very kind of Mrs Lucas.'

'Not really,' said Maria thoughtfully. Her mother stared.

'I mean it is kind . . . But they've got so many children she doesn't notice if there's an extra one anyway. And if I'm there Martin doesn't fight with Charlotte and Elisabeth. So it's quite kind to her in a way too.'

'Oh,' said Mrs Foster. And then, 'Yes, I see.' She looked at Maria with something like bewilderment and Maria turned pink and went to find her bathing costume.

There was an oppressiveness about the weather. The sky seemed to have descended until a belt of pewter cloud, matching the cliffs in colour, lay overhead, sandwiching beach, fields and town between the layers of grey sea, sky and cliffs. Maria, looking up from the carpet of shattered blue lias amid which they were currently fossil-hunting, said, 'I feel like an ammonite.'

'How?'

'Shut up in greyness.'

'It's going to rain, that's all,' said Martin sensibly.

'You know,' said Maria, 'the other day a most peculiar thing happened . . .'

Silence, if you are embarking on an important piece of information, is quite encouraging. 'We were walking,' she went on, to Martin's back view, 'along the cliff path on the other side of the town—and we went down one of the bites—you know what I mean —the places where there's been a landslip once—and I got this odd feeling . . .'

She paused for a moment and then, since Martin's back expressed no emotion either approving or disapproving, went on '. . . I got this feeling that everything was moving, like if you spin round and round with your arms out, and then stand still. But before that I kept hearing this dog yapping, only there wasn't any dog at least I couldn't see one and the others—they couldn't even hear it. And it was the same dog I've been hearing in the garden at the house, I'm sure of that.'

'I've never heard it,' said Martin. 'What dog?' He squatted down over a pile of stones, turning them over.

'Just a dog,' said Maria lamely. Like, she had been about to say, I used to hear the swing before we found it. She did not, though, say it. Instead she said abruptly, 'There'd have been landslips along there, wouldn't there—where we walked yesterday?'

'S'pose so,' said Martin. He hammered a stone in half and threw it aside.

'I think,' said Maria, 'I think I kind of got caught up in one that happened there once a long time ago. Heard it all again.'

'Don't be silly,' said Martin. He stood up and stared at the grey heights of Black Ven.

'People could have got killed in landslips, couldn't they?'

'Obviously.'

'Children . . .'

'Presumably.' He began to wander away through the gorse-bushes.

'Harriet, perhaps . . .' said Maria, but he was out of earshot now, and as she trailed after him she said to the fossil in her hand (a small *Gryphaea*, worn to a shadow by forty odd million years of time and change), I've thought so much about Harriet that sometimes I almost feel I am her. Like on the swing the other day I swung higher and higher, she said to it, and I felt as though I was changing into someone else, someone with long skirts on and thick woolly stockings and long hair, not a bit like mine. Harriet, in fact.

'We'll try over there,' said Martin.

'Yes,' said Maria, 'that looks a good place.'

It wasn't a very good place, after all, yielding nothing but an old coke tin and some bits of broken plastic.

'It's been done,' said Martin, disgusted. 'It's that man with the proper geological hammer. I wish we had one. He's always going to get things we can't. Unless we could get to places he doesn't go.' He stared round, at the shelving cliffs, the slipping, sliding landscape of the blue lias.

'Not up there!' said Maria in alarm.

'Why not?'

'It's dangerous.'

'I don't see why. I saw someone up there yesterday. It's all right if you're careful.'

'I don't think I'd like it,' said Maria. 'I feel funny when I'm up high.'

'Then I'll go by myself. I daresay,' he said casually, 'I might find a *Dapedius* up there.'

Large, warm drops of rain were beginning to fall. From down below on the beach they could hear the shouting of Mrs Lucas, rounding up children.

'Not now, I s'pose,' said Martin. 'Some time. Some time soon. It's almost the end of August. There's not much longer.'

Torrential rain fell that night. The swing creaked mournfully in the garden and Maria, infected as it were by the general dismalness of everything, lay in bed listening to it and thinking sad but vague thoughts about things moving and changing all the time and there being nothing at all you can do about it. Days run one into another, until they are last week, or last month, and they have got away and gone under your very fingers, as it were, like water in a river. It's nearly September, she thought, nearly the end of our summer

105

holiday, and then we'll be going home and all this time here will be something we've put away, like old photographs. And it'll get muzzy, like old photographs, so you can't quite remember how it was. This house, and Martin, and the swing, and the fossils, and everything.

9

Rain, and a Game of Hide-and-Seek

Next morning, the world ran with water. It coursed from the roof and found its way to the ground through drainpipes and over the rim of gutters and down the walls themselves, changed from white to grey with damp. The garden was bowed down by water, bushes drooping and flattened, the trees dripping incessantly, the grass treacherous with hidden bogs. The cat, picking its way across the lawn, lifted its sodden feet angrily and sat down on the far side, tail lashing, to stare at the birds who sat huddled on branches and telephone wires, enduring the weather. For still it rained: the view out of the window was blurred with water. Sometimes it fell heavily, in thick sheets, sometimes in misty curtains that swung across the backdrop of the garden and the houses beyond.

'Well,' said Mrs Foster. 'Not a day for the beach.'

Mr Foster removed himself to the drawing-room with the newspaper.

'A nice quiet day indoors,' said Mrs Foster with satisfaction. 'Will you be all right, darling?'

'I'm not sure,' said Maria.

'You could have a nice day reading,' said her mother comfortably. 'Or doing a jigsaw. Or playing with those fossils you've been finding.'

'I don't think I feel like reading,' said Maria. And she added, in her head, with resignation, and you don't *play* with fossils.

'Well,' said Mrs Foster, 'I'm sure you'll think of something.'

Her attention, Maria could see, was already with the patchwork quilt.

The door bell rang. Mrs Foster, peering through the window, said without great enthusiasm, 'Here's Martin,' and then, more brightly, 'I expect he's come to ask you over.'

But this was not, as it turned out, the case. Mrs Foster's face, listening to what he had to say, grew more and more dismayed. Finally he stopped, and there was a brief pause, during which both children gazed expectantly at Mrs Foster while she arranged her face into a less appalled expression.

'Well, no, Martin, of course I don't mind. No, it would be nice to have you and the girls over if your mother and your aunt want to go off for the day. And James. James is how old? Yes, I see.' The dismay came back for a moment, only rather more so, and then she went on, valiantly, 'What about the babies? They're taking the babies. Yes, well I expect that would be the best thing. Go and tell your mother to send the others over as soon as she likes.'

Martin departed with the message. Mrs Foster said to Maria, 'There now, you won't be lonely after all.' She looked sadly at her work-basket, and then went into the larder, emerging with a lot of tins to say, 'Do you think they would be happy with some kind of stew? For lunch.'

Maria said she thought they would. And then she did something she did not often do, except when going to bed, which was to kiss her mother. Mrs Foster looked surprised, kissed back, and became very busy opening tins and mixing things. 'I can't imagine how Mrs Lucas manages,' she said, 'every day. Five of them.' And then, hopefully, 'Perhaps you could all play a nice quiet board-game.'

Martin returned, along with James, Charlotte, Elisabeth and Lucy. Martin was behaving in a way that was partly irritable and partly bossy, since this was the house of his friend, which he knew well and the rest didn't. The others were inquisitive and somewhat over-excited. James instantly fell over the doormat and wept, loudly. The girls rushed hither and thither, exploring. Mr Foster put his head round the drawing-room door, took in the situation with one horri-fied glance, and retreated. Within, he could be heard hastily shutting doors and windows.

'Gosh! What a super house!'

'What shall we do?'

'Where do those stairs go to?'

'Sardines!'

'Can we go in there?'

'Hide-and-seek!'

'Oh, dear . . .' said Mrs Foster, and then, with more determination, 'not in the library, I'm afraid. Or the drawing-room. What about a game of Monopoly?'

Confronted with the silence of total lack of enthusiasm, she abandoned this proposal.

'Hide-and-seek!' said an anonymous voice.

And Martin, in his most charming and reassuring tone for the pacifying of nervous mothers, said, 'I'll see they don't do anything they oughtn't to, Mrs Foster. Shut up, all of you! I promise we won't break anything. Or disturb anyone. Honestly. You won't know we're here.'

Mrs Foster seemed not entirely convinced by this. 'Well . . .'

'They'll do exactly what I tell them,' said Martin grandly. 'Come on, you lot.' And they were gone, all the children, up the stairs, thunderously, with Maria at the back, feeling all of a sudden lively and excitable, one of them, exclaiming and suggesting with every-one else.

'I'm He,' said Martin. 'Maria's bedroom is Home. I'm counting fifty. Everywhere except the drawing-room and that library place. If anyone breaks anything I'll belt them. Right! ONE—TWO—THREE . . .'

They dispersed. They melted away, with giggles and little shrieks, into rooms and cupboards and under beds and behind curtains. Maria, crouching in the broom cupboard, heard James wandering forlorn and complaining without, and pulled him in beside her. Together they trembled happily in darkness and dust, and together they crept forth and made a bolt for it up the stairs again, converging in pandemonium upon her room, everyone shouting at once, in triumph or despair. Breathless, they sprawled in heaps upon Maria's floor until sufficiently recovered to start again. And then they dispersed . . .

The house alternated between silence and commotion. A suspended, anticipating silence, and then a creeping and a pattering of feet that swelled to a frantic dashing, a leaping of stairs and banging of doors, the howling of the hunter who has seen the hunted and the despairing shriek of the hunted who know themselves to be beyond help. And Maria, in the thick of it, found herself caught up so as to become not just one of them but barely even herself at all. She was behaving in a most un-Maria-like way. She rushed; she screamed; she pushed and giggled. She charged from room to room, skidded upon mats, hurled herself under beds. Once, leaping down the stairs with wild whoops, she and her father confronted one another in the hall, her father standing with the newspaper in his hand and the persecuted look of someone returning home to find their own street made unrecognizable by an invasion of road-works. At the sight of this transformed Maria his face took on an expression of astonishment as well and for a moment the real, everyday Maria gazed back in wonder and embarrassment before the game took charge once more and she was racing through the hall and past him, shrieking.

It was splendid fun. And then all of a sudden the mood changed. Each hunt became longer, more devious, less uproarious and more calculating. Daring gave way to stealth. They knew all the hiding-places now, and they were out of breath and becoming a little exhausted. James, sucking his thumb, curled up on Maria's bed and went to sleep. For the rest, each hiding and each seeking became longer and longer, the hunter lurking behind doors to pounce, the hunted slipping from under bed to behind chair, from the shadow of a curtain to the concealing bulk of a chest-of-drawers. The house became a listening, waiting place—a place on two levels of consciousness, one in which Mrs Foster clattered pans in the kitchen and Mr Foster once more barricaded himself into the drawing-room, and another in which five pairs of eyes and ears preyed upon each other, waiting for the betraying creak of a floor-board or flicker of movement through the crack of a door.

Maria had found a new hiding-place, and no one else knew about it. It was in the room at the end of the passage upstairs, beyond the bedrooms, not used for anything now except a lot of spare furniture, which stood awkwardly about the room in no kind of arrangement. Some of this furniture was shrouded in huge old sheets and counterpanes. The children had discarded as hiding-places the tables and ordinary upright chairs which wore such draperies over and around them like skirts: they were known now, every seeker peered beneath them as a ritual while combing this particular room. But one large squashy armchair, covered with a huge, flowery, rather torn, counterpane was so low upon the floor that it was not feasible to get underneath it. Unless, that is, you were as small and thin as Maria. Charlotte and the others, who were all inclined to stoutness, had cast one dismissive look at it. But Maria found that she could slide beneath it, inserting herself like a paperknife under its sagging springs and drawing the counterpane down to the floor around it. There, flattened dustily between the floor-boards and the underneath of the chair, she could lie as long as she liked, biding her time, while seekers came and went, twitching aside other dust-sheets, pulling back the curtains, and through a tear in the counterpane she watched their sandalled feet skitter past, hugging herself with glee. For once it was no bad thing to be smaller than other people.

They stopped coming. Everyone must be looking for her now. The house had gone very quiet. I'll wait a bit longer, she thought, till I'm sure they're all downstairs, and then I'll creep out and get Home. And thinking this she fell into a comfortable drowsiness, with the room quietly empty around her and no sound anywhere except the rain on the windows. And rather oddly, the piano, she thought, being played very faintly in the drawing-room. Which, had she been more alert and not in this somnolent state, would have seemed strange since her father did not play the piano. Moreover it was playing the tune that she had tried to play once from that old album in the piano stool.

In fact, she realized, the room was not absolutely quiet either. There was a clock ticking, which was also strange since she did not remember having seen a clock. However, peering out through that convenient tear in the counterpane, she saw it now, in the far corner, and was further surprised to find that it was the same as the one in Mrs Shand's drawing-room—the one whose face was encircled with painted flowers—violets, daisies, honeysuckle. The one whose hands had stopped forever at ten to four. But this one had not stopped: it ticked away busily there, and said five past twelve, which must be about right, Maria thought.

Getting on for lunch-time, because she could hear reassuring clatterings from the kitchen below, and there was a smell of roast mutton drifting through the open door. The chair pressed down rather uncomfortably upon her back (or else the floor was pressing upwards), more than it had done when she first got under it, almost indeed as though she had got fatter since, and instead of feeling drowsy she found herself clasping her hands over her mouth to suppress giggles. Which again was odd because Maria was not, by and large, a giggly person. But here she was squashed beneath a chair, peering out beside its brown mahogany ball-and-claw foot, stifling waves of laughter. Because she mustn't be discovered. There was a person in a long dark dress sitting at a desk in the corner over there, writing, and this person must not know she was there.

The person wrote, and the clock ticked, and downstairs someone played the piano and other people did things in the kitchen. And then the person in the long dark dress got up and went to the door and called out into the passage 'Harriet! Harriet . . . Will you come now please . . .' And, returning, she paused for a moment beside the chair so that the hem of her dress was a few inches from the nose of the watcher beneath it, which made the giggling more and more difficult to control. The person in the long dress sat down again, in a chair this time, and took something from a work-basket, which she held upon her lap and frowned at, and then tutted in irritation, and the watcher beneath the chair, at the sight of it, was swept with boredom and distaste, so that even the giggles were quelled. She stared balefully out through the fringe of stuff that hung down from the chair, and resolved to stay quiet and still and hidden for so long that she need not do her needlework, not now, not today, not ever . . . Because I'll stay here for ever and ever, she thought, they'll never find me, I'll always be here, under the chair.

And Maria, waking from what must have been a doze, with pins and needles in one leg, thought, I've been here for *hours*, for ever and ever, they've forgotten about me, they've all gone off and forgotten about me . . . And she eased herself out from under the chair into the empty room (she'd thought there was a clock just now, but that was silly, because there was no clock) and then, cautiously, into the passage.

And at just that moment there was Martin, the seeker, edging round the bathroom door, so that he spotted her at just the moment she spotted him and there was a wild dash for Home, ending in a noisy heap on her bedroom floor.

'Where were you?'

And Maria wouldn't say. I'll never say, she thought, I'll never tell anyone about that place. It's private. Private to me.

There was stew for lunch, and ice-cream. The visitors were appreciative and all talked at once. Mr and Mrs Foster, at either end of the long table in the dining-room—which they were using since the kitchen seemed too small for this occasion—tried their best to impose order upon the conversation and then gave up. Mr Foster left the table as soon as he decently could and Mrs Foster devoted herself to seeing that the food was shared out equally.

'You've got super parents,' said Charlotte, afterwards, 'they don't interrupt.'

Late that afternoon, at a point when the children were seated round the kitchen table playing snap in an atmosphere of the utmost peace and harmony, Mrs Lucas arrived to fetch them. What a relief it was, she said, to see that they had been so good and quiet, and now she knew that they *could* behave themselves if they wanted to (at this point Mr Foster began to say something and then didn't but went rather quickly out into the garden instead) she wouldn't feel bad about pushing them over again another time . . . (At this point Mrs Foster opened her mouth to speak and then managed somehow not to.) And wouldn't it be fun, Mrs Lucas went on cheerfully, to have an absolutely slap-up both-families picnic one day before the end of the holiday. A farewell picnic.

'A cooking picnic!'

'No sandwiches. Make a fire and fry things.'

'In the evening! A *night* picnic!'

'When?' said Martin.

And it was arranged, somehow, despite Mrs Foster standing there saying things like not-absolutely-sure-about-our-plans and Mr Foster coming back in from the garden and just looking horrified. A week from then, on 5 September, the last whole day. At a place the Lucases had been to off the path to Axmouth.

'Idyllic,' said Mrs Lucas, 'I can't tell you . . . Not a soul in sight. Just lots of nature. There's a bit of a climb down, of course.'

'The weather may put paid to it,' said Mrs Foster hopefully, and then was told by all the Lucas children at once that actually if they were going to have a picnic they had it anyway, whether it was raining or not. Mr Foster retreated into the garden again and the Lucases, after many false starts and sudden returns to collect forgotten jerseys, went.

The Fosters had barely settled down again on their own when the doorbell rang once more. It was Mrs Shand. Maria's father, becoming extremely genial and welcoming at the sight of someone aged well over eleven, invited her to come in for a glass of something. They all went into the drawing-room to sit and Maria found herself drawn after them, not so much because she wanted to as because she could find no appropriate moment at which to slip off on her own. Mrs Shand had a way of glancing now and then in her direction, or addressing remarks to her which could in no way be replied to.

'Well,' said Mrs Shand, 'you'll be having to think about school again soon now,' and Maria said that she supposed she would. In her mind, a large shutter came down with a thump, like the stage-curtain lowered in the interval at a theatre. 6 September, it said. Beyond it, removed and stored, stood the swing, the blue lias cliffs, grass vetchling, horsetail and burnet saxifrage, the ilex tree and Martin.

'Yes,' said Mrs Shand, 'time and tide wait for no man.' And, this being said, she looked round the room, and then at Maria again, with a certain satisfaction.

'Time was,' she went on, 'I've sat in this room myself, counting days. I was at boarding-school. I sometimes wonder, nowadays . . .' She looked again at Maria, critically, and inquired if the Fosters had never considered boarding her. Mrs Foster, just a little irritably, replied that they hadn't. And then, changing the subject, said that it must have a lot of memories for her, this house. Had it always been the family home?

'Not quite from its very beginnings,' said Mrs Shand. 'Someone else built it, in the early years of the century. The nineteenth century, you understand,' she added, to Maria, who said nothing but assumed her cold look, and wondered if Mrs Shand knew that ammonites are about a hundred and forty million years old, and that trilobites, being older yet, are not found in the blue lias. And that the ilex is a kind of oak tree. I am not stupid, she said, inside her head.

'Its appearance has changed, of course. My father had the brickwork plastered over.'

'That's why it's brown in the sampler?' said Maria.

'Of course.'

'I found the swing, Harriet's swing.'

Mrs Shand looked over the sofa, and out into the garden. 'So I see.'

'We painted it.'

'I should perhaps have mentioned . . . began Mrs Foster. 'I do hope you . . .'

'That is perfectly all right,' said Mrs Shand.

'Whose is the dog?' said Maria. 'The one that keeps barking in the garden?' The question came out so abruptly as to sound rude. She had not intended this: it was merely what happened when she was interested in something. Out of the corner of her eye, she saw her father look disapproving.

'There is no dog that I know of,' said Mrs Shand. 'Not in this house. My family has had a habit of keeping cats, for a long time now.'

The next question rose to Maria's lips. It floated, unspoken, so that is seemed to her that it must hang from her mouth like bubble-speech in a cartoon. '*What happened to Harriet?*'

She said nothing.

Mrs Shand took a sip of sherry and looked out of the window again, over the garden at the leaden sea, huddled beneath a sullen sky. 'I fear there is more rain on the way.'

'Depressing weather,' said Mr Foster.

'An excess of rain is always worrying on this coast,' said Mrs Shand, 'things being what they are.'

'You mean,' said Maria, 'it makes there be landslips?'

'Precisely.'

'It *causes* landslips,' said Mr Foster, 'Not "it makes there be".'

There was a silence. Mrs Shand finished her glass of sherry. The cat, who had slid through the door in time to hear the last part of the conversation, gave Maria a patronizing look, and twined itself lovingly around Mrs Shand's legs.

'I must go,' said Mrs Shand. 'We dine at seven-thirty.'

She had been right about the rain. Having held off throughout a grey and brooding evening, it began again as soon as darkness fell. Maria, lying in bed, heard it rustling on the roof of the garage, a steady, rhythmic noise that should have been soothing but somehow was not, so that when at last she fell asleep it was to dream, disturbingly, wake, and dream again. And in her dreams things were not as they should be, the world became an unstable and uncertain place, nothing could be relied upon. She walked across a green and solid lawn, but the lawn collapsed beneath her feet like the scummy surface of a duck-pond, and she went plunging down through bottomless skies that had the thick grey texture of cloud. She waited outside her school for her mother, but the person who came to fetch her was a little old woman, smaller than herself, who nevertheless spoke with her mother's voice. She opened the front door of her own home, but beyond it, instead of the carpeted hall, with table and mirror above, was a gently lapping sea, beneath whose glassy surface there swam ammonites in shoals, *Gryphaea* and *Promicroceras* and the rest. And when at last she escaped from these unsettling places, it was to plod down endless streets in search of something that she had lost but could not identify—some book or purse—and which she knew she could never find again. She woke up in the morning irritable and unrested.

10

The Picnic

The rain was followed by several sullen and overcast days. It became cold. People said—with irritating predictability—that you could feel autumn in the air. And Maria, exasperated, shut her ears to them, partly because she disliked people to say what she had known they were going to say but mostly because she did not want to be reminded of this. She did not want autumn to come; she did not want to go home to London; she wanted each day to stretch like elastic and indeed preferably for the following day not to arrive at all. She was enjoying herself. Perhaps it had been something to do with the game of hide-and-seek, or perhaps it was the swing, which was so much regarded now as her personal property that everyone referred to it as Maria's swing. Perhaps it was (she wondered herself, secretly) that she was mysteriously changing into a somewhat different person. The fact was, though, that for the first time in her life she felt quite remarkably at ease with other people. Not only with Martin but also with Charlotte and Elisabeth and Lucy and various others with whom they played. She and Martin went off less on their own together. Instead, elaborate and complicated games took place for a great many people, organized by Martin, and in which Maria found herself occupying some kind of privileged position, as though he were a king and she his favourite minister. She became, for her, positively noisy, interrupting other people and making suggestions. She found that she could giggle with Charlotte. She did not wait for people to invite her to join in but simply did so, and nobody seemed to mind or think it strange. It was all rather surprising.

And all the while time was leaking away. There were ten days left, and then a week, and then the days lay ahead singly, five and four and three. And as they went Maria found herself overwhelmed with the most peculiar anxiety. It was not just that she did not want the holiday to end, but that she felt also a strong sense of apprehension. She felt that something was going to happen, but she did not know what it was or when it would be. And she did not think it would be something nice. She became jumpy and nervous. The sudden slam of a door made her heart rocket most unpleasantly. The cat, sliding against her leg under the table as she wrote, made her drop the pencil.

'Don't *do* that.'

'Sorry, I'm sure,' said the cat, rasping its tongue against her ankle, a disagreeable feeling. 'It's my nature, you must remember. The stealthy movement of the hunter.'

'Fat lot of hunting you do,' snapped Maria.

'No need, is there? Not with eighteen different kinds of pet-food on the market. But old habits die hard. Deep down,' it went on, theatrically, 'I'm remembering my savage ancestors, padding around those forests and jungles after their prey. I have to keep my hand in. It's my nature, as I said.'

'You should control yourself,' said Maria.

'And I thought you were so well-informed about evolution and all that. Anyway, who's talking? What about you and your friends, up and down that tree all day, just like a lot of monkeys. Your ancestors aren't anything to write home about.'

'That's entirely different. We do it because it's fun.'

'Huh . . .' said the cat. 'And in any case, what's the matter with you these days? You're like a cat on hot bricks, if you'll pardon the expression.'

'I don't know. I feel nervous. I keep thinking about Harriet.'

120

'Harriet, my dear child, lived over a hundred years ago. She doesn't exist any more. Be your age.' It yawned, pinkly.

'I know' said Maria. 'I know all that. But you see,' she went on, 'I think she does in a way. Because of places being like clocks—full of all the time there's ever been in them, and all the people, and all the things that have happened, like the ammonites in the stones. You don't know what I'm talking about, do you?'

'To be absolutely frank,' said the cat, 'no'. There was a rattle of plates from the kitchen below and it stretched itself and strolled out of the door and down the stairs.

Maria stared out of the window at the dark bulk of the ilex tree. I could have asked Mrs Shand what happened to Harriet, she thought. But somehow I couldn't. I suppose I didn't really want to be told.

If you ask blunt questions you get blunt answers, and the whole matter of Harriet was far too delicate and personal for that. If it weren't for actual, real things like the sampler, and the initials on the table in her room, and, come to that, the swing, she could almost think that she'd invented her, or imagined her. Always, since she was quite small, Maria had been extremely confused between what she had imagined and what was real, so much so that she had learned to keep quiet about a good many things in case they turned out (like that burglar) to be part of the imaginings, so that everybody stared at you and you felt extremely foolish. Frequently, she was unsure whether she had thought things or actually said them out loud. Lately, she seemed to have been saying almost as much as thinking, which was un-Maria-like and part, she suspected, of this odd process of changing into someone a little different. Although, when you considered the matter, it was not really so very odd. Since people change on the outside all the time—first growing bigger year by year, going from baby to child and then to grown-up, and then getting wrinkles, and their hair turning grey—it seemed reasonable enough that they might also be changing inside, in how they felt and thought and behaved.

'Mrs Lucas has just reminded me,' said Maria's mother, coming into the kitchen, 'about this picnic. I don't quite see,' she went on, regretfully, 'how we are to get out of it.'

'I know,' said Maria. 'It's tomorrow.' And the day after, she thought, we are going.

'But not in the evening,' Mrs Foster continued, 'even Mrs Lucas thought that was a bad idea. A lunch picnic.'

'We're going to cook everything ourselves. No sandwiches.'

'That seems to be the plan,' said Mrs Foster hopelessly.

Part of Maria was looking forward to the picnic. Part of her, though, was dreading it. The day after, they would go. And thinking of this all that morning, down on the beach, under sombre skies that threatened rain, with the wet sand chill under her feet, she became silent, more like the old Maria, and hung at the edges of the games, and finally did not want to play any more but went up early to the house, leaving the others. And that evening, alone in the garden in the twilight, she swung and swung, going higher and higher until the swing rocked a little on its black iron legs, and again Harriet was so strongly in her head that the thought of her seemed to blur the real world and alter sounds and feelings so that she, Maria, might momentarily have been someone else, some time else.

She woke next morning to a day of wind, racing clouds and sunshine. Mrs Foster, whose hopes had been pinned to appalling weather and a forced last-minute cancellation of the picnic, stared dourly out of the window and set off for the grocer's to buy sausages. Mr Foster, who had made a desperate but unsuccessful bid to get out of the whole thing by pleading a sudden chill, began to assemble rugs and a vast supply of matches and firelighters. Martin arrived in the middle of this and depressed him even further with tales of other picnics that the Lucases had had along the same lines in the past, packed with drama and disaster. Surreptitiously, Mr Foster added Dettol, sticking-plaster and bandages to his expanding pile of equipment. Mrs Foster returned from the shops with food that Martin examined with appreciation.

'Super nosh . . . Once,' he began reflectively, 'we roasted an ox on Wandsworth Common. Well, not really an ox—a leg of lamb from Sainsbury's but it was the same idea. That was the time James got his head stuck between those iron railings.' Mr Foster picked up the newspaper and retreated into the drawing-room.

At last, after many comings and goings to fetch items that had been forgotten by way of food, drink, clothing and various small Lucas children, both families assembled on the drive in front of the house. The Fosters were dressed for every eventuality of weather, wore sensible walking shoes, and carried their possessions in convenient bags and baskets. The Lucases were clad in everything from bathing-suits to what appeared to be some kind of fancy dress, and clutched innumerable tattered carrier-bags which leaked chops, sausages, tea-bags and the odd can of beer (which Mrs Foster eyed with disapproval). Martin's mother carried nothing except a baby and a book. The older children were weighed down with everything from fishing-tackle to beach-balls. They made a most ill-assorted party, which was apparently what Mrs Shand thought, passing the gateway and staring in at them with unconcealed curiosity.

'An outing of some kind, I see.'

'We're going for a picnic,' said Mrs Foster bravely.

'To Charmouth, no doubt?'

There was a chorus of contempt from the Lucas children.

'Not just the ordinary *beach*.'

'A special place of ours . . .'

'That way . . .'

'You have to climb down *miles*.'

'It's all lovely and slippery.'

'Ever so steep . . .'

Mrs Shand listened with what seemed particular attention. And Maria, watching her, felt again this creep of unease and apprehension that was blighting what should otherwise be a most agreeable, indeed a thoroughly special and extraordinary day. She had never, after all, done this kind of thing before: Foster picnics were invariably matters of thermoses and foil-wrapped sandwiches, eaten at carefully selected and unhazardous places. But Mrs Shand, staring at them over her spectacles, brought back other thoughts and she found herself, suddenly, wishing that they could do something entirely different. Just stay here, for instance. And thinking that, knew it to be impossible, even if someone as small and uninfluential as herself could persuade all those other people, louder and older. There is a point at which a certain train of events is begun, and nothing in the world can stop it, and one is caught up in it and part of it, willy-nilly.

'Mmn . . .' said Mrs Shand, and then, 'well, I should take care, if I were you.'

'Why?' said Maria, and although the question was drowned in an outbreak of talk from the Lucases, and no one paid any attention, it somehow reached Mrs Shand, for she looked directly at Maria and said, 'For obvious reasons.'

'Obvious . . .?' Nobody was listening. James had fallen over and grazed his knee. Piercing screams swamped everything.

'The cliffs along there are notoriously unsafe. There was a tragedy in the past—many years ago now. However, I'm sure you are all extremely competent.' And Mrs Shand was gone, stumping away down the road, leaving Maria staring after her, the question she would have liked to ask left unspoken, echoing only in her head.

What tragedy?

'Off we go,' said Martin's mother. 'Not before time. Oh, be quiet, James, you're not dead yet. Jane, you've dropped a sausage.'

They straggled away down the track beyond the garden and over the fields towards the cliff path. Mr Foster, with a sudden assumption of command, as the only man of the party, took the lead but was rapidly overtaken by rushing, competing Lucas children. He strode along behind them, occasionally calling warnings which were ignored, and presently lapsed into a glum silence, recognizing that things were out of control. The rest of the party, women and small children, trailed along behind. Maria, last of all, followed reluctantly. She was carrying a bag heavy with cups and the plates, knives and forks which she had known to be unsuitable but which Mrs Foster had insisted upon packing.

'They eat with their fingers, the Lucases.'

'I daresay they do.' Maria wished she were back in the kitchen, having that conversation with her mother.

By the time they reached the start of the cliff path several children were missing. There was a long stop while they were rounded up. Mr Foster sat on a stile and stared out to sea in silence. Finally, with the party reassembled they set off once more, along the narrow woodland path that meant they must walk in single file. The Lucas children, pushing and shoving each other, rushed off at a gallop, all trying to be first. Mr Foster, abandoning all attempts at leadership, placed himself last of all, presumably to gather up the lost or injured. The various sections of the party soon became separated, though clearly audible to each other as their voices came through the trees. Maria, hanging back from the rest of the children, could hear their progress marked by the woodpigeons that erupted from the branches as they approached, and the occasional shriek of a jay.

They went on and on. They passed the point at which the Fosters had turned back on that Saturday afternoon walk with Aunt Ruth and Uncle David. Maria, plodding onward, could imagine her mother's misgivings, and felt a flicker of sympathy. Mostly, though, she was buried in her own thoughts and feelings. They had reached

125

a part of the woods where the trees were of the most immense size, towering above her to such heights that, straining her neck to look up at them, they seemed to crowd out the sky altogether. She felt even smaller than usual. Putting her hand on the trunk of a huge beech, as far up as she could, she was covering only a minute fraction of its height; far above her, the leaves shivered and rustled indifferently. They must be very old trees, these. Hundreds of years old, indeed. Perhaps Harriet had walked underneath them and had the same feelings of smallness and insignificance. Perhaps she too had felt dizzy as she looked upwards at those shifting branches, had wished herself somewhere more open, less silent and oppressive.

The silence, though, was partly her own creation, removed into her own thoughts. For, coming round a corner, she caught up suddenly with the other children, engaged in ferocious discussion that rang through the trees.

'It's down here.'

'No, it isn't. You don't know *anything*. It's further.'

'It's *here*. I remember that tree.'

'There was a sort of path ...'

'Shut up, you lot,' said Martin, authoritatively. 'It's there. We'll have to wait for the others. *Mum ...* !'

Gradually, they all regathered. Maria observed with amazement that her father was now carrying a small child (she never could remember all their names). He looked exhausted and his hair was much disarranged on one side where the baby was strap-hanging from it.

'Down there?' said Mrs Foster in alarm.

The path, at this point, followed what must really be a ledge along steeply shelving cliffs. To one side, the ground reared upwards to where, above and through the trees, the final rocky summit of the cliff could be seen, golden-brown, capped with turf and bushes. And to the other it dropped away down to some invisible point where the sea could be heard washing to and fro on the shingle. But, thick with trees and undergrowth as this place was, it seemed not so much cliff as woodland that had somehow got tipped on one side. It was only looking downwards, at the thin track plunging away through bushes, that you realized how steep it was.

'I wonder if perhaps . . .' began Mrs Foster.

But nobody paid any attention to what she might have had to say. The Lucas children were explaining that there was a proper beach at the bottom and nobody ever went there so you had it all to yourself. ('So I should imagine,' said Mr Foster drily). And, they insisted, it wasn't half as steep as it looked, and all started plunging one after another down this precipitous path (that barely seemed certain if it was indeed a path) while behind the mothers shouted, 'Be careful! Not so *fast*!' and somewhere a long way below the sea pushed and pulled uncaringly on the pebbles.

They descended, one after another, each intent upon his or her own self-preservation. Except, of course for the mothers, who each felt burdened with a great many safeties, according to the fate of mothers, and were in states of anxiety which varied according to their personalities—in other words, noisily but only mildly concerned in the case of the Lucas mothers, silent and in a near-frenzy in the case of Mrs Foster. Maria put one foot slowly and carefully in front of the other, steadying herself with a hand on a sapling or jutting rock where possible. Once she skidded on some treacherous shale that slithered under her shoes, so that she sat down hard, bruising herself. It could have been worse. Below and out of sight, hair-raising cries from the other children suggested fatal accidents of one kind or another. Mr Foster, still encumbered with the baby, came down with deliberate care and slowness, beyond doing anything except (presumably) hope for the best.

At last they were all down and there, as promised, was a beach. Though not, at first sight, a beach very much different from any other except that, also as promised, there was no one else in sight.

Otherwise, it seemed a long and arduous way to have come for a minor change of scenery. Maria, looking at her mother, could feel her thinking this.

Instantly, there was a great deal to be done. Driftwood had to be collected for a fire. A hearth had to be built from stones, with wind-break. The fire had to be built, and kept stoked. Cooking had to be started. It all took a great deal of time and argument among the Lucases. Mrs Foster, who was used to eating at one o'clock sharp, watched discontentedly as the hands of her watch crept past two. Maria wandered about, collecting anything that would burn from the line of seaweed and rubbish that wavered along the shingle. The others were all squabbling—though no more so, perhaps, than usual—over who should do what and eat what. The mothers made decisions and cooked. Mr Foster stood around, trying to stop children from getting too near the fire. Maria felt very detached from everyone else: she had hardly spoken to anyone for hours, and no one seemed to miss her, except Martin, who said kindly, once, 'Are you feeling sick or something?' She shook her head and pretended to be much involved with breaking up a decaying wooden box.

The fact was that she did feel rather peculiar. Not exactly ill, but all on edge. Her legs were shaky (though this might perhaps be accounted for by the long walk, followed by the steep descent). Continuing to dismantle the box, so that she should be left alone and not chivvied to help in some way, she sat with her back to the sea—that fretful grey surface somehow made her feel even more uneasy—and looked at the cliffside down which they had come. But that, mantled in swaying trees, was as unsteady as the sea. Only here and there did it seem solid, where areas of bared rock and soil showed, uncovered yet by greenery. Most of the greenery, as she now knew, was old, ancient . . . Immense trees. Roots like serpents jutting from the ground. Ferns. Jungly plants. Everything grows and grows, she thought, everywhere, all the time, leaves and stalks

128

and flowers and seeds . . . Anything could be happening—people getting born and dying and being happy or not happy—but they don't care, they just go on growing and growing. And, thinking this, the shouts of the other children, the pop-pop of a motor-boat somewhere out to sea, the whimper of Martin's baby sister, seemed drowned by a deafening imaginary sound of vegetable pods cracking open. The beach and the sea and the cliff became a mindless place of rock and plant and tree and the ceaselessly foraging gulls. It could have been any time; thousands of years ago, or yesterday. Or about 1865.

'Maria . . . ! Don't you want something to eat?'

She joined the circle round the fire, but she was a part of it in person only. She ate a sausage in her fingers, and heard them talking, and saw the fire's hot and treacherous bed of black ash. And above the fire to a height of a couple of feet there hung and shimmered a haze of heat with the silken look of water, that distorted slightly whatever was beyond it so that Charlotte's round pink face, blissfully munching at her chop, quivered and became blurred. And presently it was not Charlotte's face at all, but Harriet's face, and Maria sat and stared at it, and thought, and wondered, and became further and further removed from the picnic.

She came out of this trance, finally, to find everyone busy clearing things away. Mr Foster had removed himself a short distance and was staring at the sea. The children were setting out an elaborate game with pebbles and piles of seaweed. All, that is, except Martin.

'Where's Martin?' said Maria.

At first nobody paid any attention. Then his mother said vaguely, 'Yes, where has Martin got to?'

Charlotte said, 'He went off by himself. He was in a mood.'

'Oh, well . . .' said Mrs Lucas. She turned over on to her stomach and opened a book.

Maria began to search the beach. First by just looking, and then by getting up and running around it in what, even in the process of doing so, she realized to be a panic-stricken and silly manner. Getting out of breath would not help. Her heart thumped and banged. It did not take long to establish that Martin was not on the beach. It was a small beach, ending at one side in some rocks and fading away at the other into the scrub-covered foot of a rather nasty-looking cliff.

'He isn't *anywhere* . . .'

Mrs Lucas rolled over and sat up. 'No,' she said, 'he isn't, is he?'

'Trust our Martin,' said the other Mrs Lucas, with a sigh. Though both looked, now faintly disturbed, but not very.

'Well,' said Mr Foster, joining them, 'I suppose we must be thinking of the homeward journey.'

Mrs Foster began to pack their things, firmly.

Maria said, in a voice on the edge of something—tears or fury or what, one could not say—that made everyone look at her, 'Martin's disappeared. He's *gone*.'

'Martin . . .' yelled his mother. She, too, started to collect possessions.

'The tide's coming in,' said Charlotte. 'P'raps Martin went round past those rocks. There isn't any beach there when the tide's high.'

'Don't be such an alarmist,' said her mother. 'Shut up and help get those cups. *Martin* . . .'

Maria turned her back on the sea, because tide or no tide, rocks or no rocks, that was not where he would be, she somehow knew. She looked at the cliff, that bare, abrupt cliff to the left, too steep for anything to grow, crumbling, it seemed, even as you looked. And that was where, if anywhere in this place, would be fossils. *Dapedius* and belemnites and the black teeth of sharks.

'He's up there!' she cried, nearly hysterical, 'I know he is!'

Everybody looked. 'Oh, heavens!' said Mrs Lucas, 'I hope not.'

'Maria,' said her father, 'what is the matter with you? How do you know? Did you see him go up there?'

Maria could only shake her head and mumble. She was shivering all over. Now they were all looking at her, not at the cliff.

'What is the matter with you, dear?' said her mother. 'He's probably just gone on ahead, hasn't he?'

'No!' said Maria, frantic. 'He's up there, on the cliff. They all are. Can't you hear the dog barking?' And it seemed unbelievable that they could not, but all stood round her in that stupid way, doing nothing, while up there, somewhere in the bushes, the poor thing was working itself into a frenzy, and now, as she listened, she could hear that heaving, shifting noise again, and above it, surely, a child's voice shouting.

'Harriet!' she said, but only in a whisper now. 'Oh, poor Harriet . . .' And as she looked at the cliff, seemingly more clothed in trees and scrub now than a few moments ago, the whole thing trembled and shook and then, most horribly, before her very eyes, slid downwards. And the noise that that little dog was making stopped, abruptly.

She put her hands in front of her eyes and burst into tears.

Everybody was talking at once, and making comforting noises. Through them she heard her mother ('. . . terribly strung up lately, for some reason. I thought it would all end in tears.') and Charlotte ('She can have my cake for tea, actually') and then someone else ('Here's Martin. Where *have* you been, for heaven's sake?').

'There now,' said Mr Foster, intensely embarrassed. 'Pull yourself together, Maria. Martin's perfectly all right.'

And Maria, taking her hand from her eyes and tear-streaked face, burst out in anguish, 'I know he's all right. It wasn't him, it was Harriet. The cliff slipped down and Harriet was killed.'

Somebody said, 'But the cliff hasn't slipped, Maria. Nothing happened at all.'

'Not now,' she wailed. 'Not now, not today. Then, back then, when Harriet was here. Oh, this is a beastly place, I hate it, it doesn't *care*. I want to go home.' And she began to run, stumbling, towards the path.

11

A Small Black Dog and One Final Piece of Blue Lias

'I trust you enjoyed the picnic,' said Mrs Shand.

'No,' said Maria, 'I didn't very much.'

It was evening. There had been the return from the picnic, of which Maria had hardly been aware, and then there had been good-byes and sortings-out of possessions, and then Maria had gone up to her room. Her parents were treating her in a gingerly fashion, with sympathy rather than irritation, as though she were mildly ill. Her mother said she thought an early night would be a good idea. Her father clearly wished to forget the whole day as soon as possible and had set about packing up for the return to London, with deliberate briskness. Maria sat on the edge of her bed for about ten minutes, and then went downstairs again.

'I thought I'd say goodbye to the landlady.'

'Yes,' said Mrs Foster in surprise. 'Yes, that would be a nice idea.'

And so there she was sitting once again on Mrs Shand's rose-covered chintz sofa, surrounded by the ticking of the clocks, urgent or ponderous according to their temperament, and looking again, and even more intently, at the sampler.

'Have you got hay-fever?' said Mrs Shand.

'No,' said Maria. And then, with a further burst of honesty, 'I've been crying.'

'How very foolish,' said Mrs Shand. 'Have a chocolate.'

'I don't really like chocolates, actually.'

Mrs Shand peered at her embroidery, and made a tutting noise. She began to unpick something with a pair of scissors. 'And why were you crying, may I ask?'

There was a pause. Mrs Shand unpicked blue silk stitches and Maria stared first at her and then at the sampler. At last she said, 'We went for a picnic at that place along the coast where there's been landslips. I didn't like it. It's a horrid place. That's where Harriet was killed, isn't it?' Her eyes filled with tears.

Mrs Shand put down her scissors. She tweaked some loose threads out of the canvas and said, 'What an extraordinary idea. Of course she wasn't.'

The tears plopped on to the knees of Maria's jeans. 'What?' she said.

Mrs Shand fished inside her sleeve and produced a white handkerchief initialled H.S. in one corner. 'You had better borrow this. Of course Harriet wasn't killed. Whatever put such an idea into your head?'

Maria scrubbed at her eyes. Her rather grand feelings of tragedy and grief were reduced suddenly to foolishness. And surprise.

'There are no pictures of her. Older, or grown-up.'

'Yes, there are,' said Mrs Shand. She pointed to a photograph in a silver frame standing on the desk.

'I never noticed that one,' said Maria. She looked at it. It showed a woman of around her mother's age and a girl of about ten or eleven. The woman wore a long skirt, clamped round her middle with a wide belt, and a blouse with a high tight neck and long sleeves. Her hair was piled up on top of her head like a bun. She had a wide, cheerful smile and was holding a basket of apples or something which she would appear just to have picked. The girl was also carrying a basket, and had a rather stern expression. She wore a sunbonnet.

'We were in Devon,' said Mrs Shand, 'some family holiday. Aunts and cousins and everyone. We were always a very tribal family.'

134

Maria gazed at the picture. 'The girl is you?'

'The girl is me.'

'And the grown-up person is . . . Harriet?'

'My aunt Harriet. Mrs Stanton. She never had any daughters of her own, only boys, so I was by way of being something of a favourite. She was,' Mrs Shand went on, with an odd note in her voice, 'a particularly nice aunt.' She picked up her sewing again.

'And then there was the sampler being finished by Susan. Harriet's sampler.'

'That was an act of charity. My aunt hated sewing and my mother was rather good at it. I do not know, frankly, why Aunt Harriet was allowed to get away with that, but somehow she was.'

'But there weren't any more photographs of her in the album. With Susan and the others.'

'She was sent to boarding-school, being considered in need of discipline. And then she married young and was out in India for a considerable time. It is just chance, that there are no more pictures.'

'I see,' said Maria.

But, she thought, and could not bring herself to say it, there is also the matter of the swing. I somehow knew there was a swing even before I saw it on the sampler, and I kept hearing this little dog barking. Or, she said to herself sternly, I kept imagining I heard this dog barking.

'Of course,' said Mrs Shand, 'there was a landslip. When Aunt Harriet was around your age. You are perfectly correct about that. And there was a minor tragedy. A sad little accident. I mentioned it to you this morning, I think, as you were about to set off.'

Maria stopped tracing the shape of the roses on the sofa with her finger and said, 'You didn't say exactly. And I thought . . .'

'You thought I was speaking of Harriet? How very unfortunate. Then I must apologize for not being more precise. No. It was not

135

that at all. They had gone fossil-hunting somewhere along the cliff-path to the west of the town. And there was a small landslip (you can still see the place, I'm told), from which happily the children were able to scramble clear, but their little dog—a little black creature they had, called Fido—was swept away and drowned. They were all much distressed.'

There was a pause. Mrs Shand rethreaded a needle and Maria sat in a tumultuous private silence and thought, so that is what it was, so now I know .. . . . I did imagine it, but in a way, too, I didn't. There *was* a dog, and something *did* happen, but not the something I thought. At last she said, 'It could have been Harriet. Who was killed, I mean.'

'Oh, yes,' said Mrs Shand, 'it could have been. Things always could have been otherwise. The fact of the matter is that they are not. What has been, has been. What is, is.' She stabbed the needle confidently into the brown canvas.

'I suppose so,' said Maria. 'But it's a very difficult thing to get used to.'

'One does eventually,' said Mrs Shand, 'there being no other choice.'

'I partly imagined it all,' said Maria. 'I do imagine things a bit.' She looked again at the photograph. Mrs Harriet Stanton, somebody's mother (and aunt) gave her a nice friendly smile.

'Evidently,' said Mrs Shand. 'No doubt you'll grow out of it.'

And grow up into somebody else, like Harriet, thought Maria. I'm not stuck at now any more than she was. And into her head came the idea of mysterious and interesting future Marias, larger and older, doing things one could barely picture. They seemed like friends she had not yet met. Harriet became Mrs Harriet Stanton, she thought (a bit stout, with sons) and I'll end up as somebody quite different too, but in a funny way we both go on being here for ever, aged ten or eleven one summer, because we once were. I like that.

136

Mrs Shand's quietly muttering transistor radio bleeped six times and said that it was eight o'clock, reminding Maria that she had better go. They said goodbye to one another with quite a lot of warmth. Mrs Shand said that she hoped perhaps she'd see them down here another year, and Maria said that she hoped so too, and then finally she turned to go. As she reached the door Mrs Shand said, 'The dog's grave is at the back of the shrubbery in the garden. Or it was when I was a child.'

'The dog that was drowned?'

'Yes. Its body was washed up on the beach and ceremoniously buried by the children. An odd idea.'

'I don't think so,' said Maria.

Because that is what I would have done, she thought, crossing the road on her way back to the house. If it had been my black dog and I was fond of it. That would have been respectful. And she thought of them—Harriet and Susan, but Harriet mostly—ceremoniously burying the dog and weeping, presumably, all the time. And with the thought sympathetic tears pricked her eyes.

Back at the house, she went straight round into the garden. It was getting late now; down by the harbour the street lights had been switched on and made long shimmering yellow ribbons across the dark water. In the garden, trees and bushes were still and black. Only the ilex rustled and whispered high up at its top. In the house lights were on; Mrs Foster moved across the kitchen window.

Maria plunged straight into the shrubbery. She worked her way along, on hands and knees mostly, passing the place where she had found the swing. Since she did not really know what she expected to find (a hump in the ground? a cross, even, maybe, a wooden cross?) her progress was rather slow. And when she had almost reached the foot of the ilex tree, where the shrubbery ended, without finding anything, she began to feel cheated. And then suddenly, sticking up among the limbs of some neglected shrub, there it was. A tombstone. A small, grey-blue slab of stone (blue lias, of course . . .).

There was something written on it. Respectfully, Maria brushed aside leaves and twigs and knelt to read. The lettering had been cut into the stone by some competent hand (they had to get someone to do that for them, she thought, that must have been quite a problem, getting the stone, and then finding a person who could do that . . .). 'FIDO', she read, 'Perished 5 Sept 1865. In fond memory of a faithful friend. H.J.P. and S.M.P.'

It was, of course September the fifth today.

She came out of the shrubbery and walked slowly back across the lawn, stopping first to pat the scaly trunk of the ilex tree, in some kind of farewell ceremony. Somehow, she did not think she would see it again. It was always possible, of course, that they might indeed come back here another year. But something told her, some new wisdom about the way things are that she seemed just now to have acquired, that even if they did, it would not be the same. I would have moved on a year, she thought, and I wouldn't be quite the same person and I mightn't think the same things at all. I mightn't, she thought, be interested in the swing and the ilex tree any more. Or Harriet. So it is nice to make the most of it while I am.

She sat for a moment on the step of the terrace, to have a last look at the lights rippling on the harbour. Beyond the end of the Cobb, a little boat with winking red and green lights puttered steadily out to sea. Along the horizon, an aeroplane had left the thin white scrawl of a vapour trail against the lemon-coloured evening sky. She could hear the steady wash of the sea on the shore, rolling pebbles on pebbles. Pebbles of blue lias, through some of which there streamed ammonites, *Gryphaea* and *Asteroceras* and the rest. The place was settling down for the night, as it had done many, many times before, without her, and as it would do again tomorrow without her, after she had gone. Places pay no attention at all, she thought, they are just there and that is all there is to it. And, thinking that, she looked fondly at this place she now knew, as you look at a person, a friend.

The cat sat down beside her, disposed, it seemed, for a chat.

138

'No,' said Maria, 'I don't think I'm going to let you talk any more. Sometimes you say uncomfortable things. Though actually,' she went on, 'I think I am getting a bit better at not being made uncomfortable. Not that you care, though, do you?' She tickled its ear, and the cat rolled on its back, purring, and then appeared to go to sleep.

She sat for a moment or two longer, listening. She was listening, in fact, for something in particular, but there was nothing to be heard except the ordinary and appropriate noises of the place—cars and people, waves and wind and seagulls. The swing was quite silent now (though it stood there still, in the middle of the lawn) and so was the little dog. I don't think I would hear them again, she thought, even if I were staying and not going home tomorrow. She went into the house.

'There you are,' said Mrs Foster. 'I was beginning to wonder.' And then she said, 'Well, home tomorrow. Quite a nice holiday, one way and another.'

And Maria said, with a most un-Maria-like vehemence, '*I think it's been a perfectly lovely holiday.*'

'Oh,' said her mother, surprised. 'Good.'

Maria sat down on the edge of the table. She watched her mother packing things up, books and clothes and her sewing-basket with the patchwork quilt. And the sight of the patchwork quilt prompted the thought that a person who is interested in patchwork quilts might also be interested in Victorian samplers, and so she began to tell her mother about Harriet's sampler. Did you know, she said, that a hundred years ago girls the same age as me had to sew these pictures? Because I've seen one that's got ammonites on it instead of flowers— sewn ammonites—and an ilex tree and a little black dog and a picture of this house. There was this girl, you see, called Harriet, in fact she grew up and became somebody's aunt, which is funny because I thought of her somehow being my age for ever and ever . . .

And her mother, instead of getting on with the packing, was so

139

distracted by this conversational, informative Maria, that the books and the sewing-basket stayed where they were, littering the table. Maria talked, and her mother listened and made sounds of interest and curiosity, and beyond them on the other side of the window night fell on Lyme Regis.